Hugs!
Laue Hayes
xo

OUT IN THE DEEP

LANE HAYES

For Brett and Claire, my water polo kids-
Your discipline, determination, and boundless energy in the water has always been an inspiration. We're endlessly proud of your accomplishments. The future is bright and it's yours for the taking.

1

"The deeper the waters are, the more still they run."—Korean proverb

MIST ROSE from the placid water, lending an ethereal aura to the foggy morning. The stands were sparsely populated at this hour. An eight a.m. Saturday game was a tough sell for most people in the summer, especially for a glorified scrimmage. There should have been a rule stating that all non-crucial collegiate events were banned until after noon in the summertime. Or maybe year-round. I glanced at our crosstown rivals at the opposite end of the pool, lined up on either side of the goal.

Water polo was an insular sport with a strong presence in coastal communities like Southern California. Chances were good that if you'd played in high school and college, you knew the competition well. I recognized the Panthers' goalie first. Jake was a fifth-year senior like me. We'd been friends since high school. He was six foot five with a wingspan that rivaled a professional basketball player's. My gaze wandered to Mike Hoskins, on

Jake's left. He was a big partier. I bet he was out late last night and no doubt, he had a hangover. Not a morning threat, I mused. Tim Berkus was slow to start, but he ramped up quickly and—*oh, fuck.* I forgot about Gabe Chadwick. I fucking hated that guy. I wasn't a fan of anyone who believed they were God's gift to humanity. So what if he was tall, dark, good-looking, smart, and a world-class athlete? Gabe was still a dick if you asked me.

And it looked like I was guarding him this morning. *Great.*

Adrenaline rushed through me when the ref blew his whistle, signaling the start of the game. I checked the tie on my cap, then swam into position and waited to see who won the sprint. Us. I moved closer to the net on the far right side and waved my hand. The second the ball was passed to me, I threw a cross-cage skip shot and scored just before Gabe reached over, pulling me under in a blatant attempt to drown me.

Okay, fine. That was a slight exaggeration. But only a slight one. Gabe yanked me sideways and then pushed me under. It was excessive force and as I held my breath and stared at his enviable six-pack underwater, I figured it was a matter of seconds before the ref called a foul. I popped back up when I realized I wasn't going to get the call and retaliated by kicking Gabe in the stomach, then swimming partially over him before getting into position on defense.

Like any other sport, the main objective in water polo was to score. The team with the most points won. In that way it was a lot like basketball or soccer. I'd been told that it looked much easier, which always made me laugh 'cause water polo was fucking vicious. Maybe it seemed like keep-away above water, but underneath it was like football. Anything was legal as long you didn't get caught. The best players knew how to get away with murder. And Gabe was definitely one of the best.

A pissed-off Gabe meant trouble for me. By the third quarter, he was all over me. I'd been kicked in the ribs, the head, and scored on twice. But I somehow managed to hang in the game, jockeying and battling for position and making it difficult for Gabe to maneuver around me. Maybe it was inevitable that he'd lose his cool and "accidentally" kick me in the balls. He grazed my left nut. It didn't actually hurt, but after getting the crap beaten out of me nonstop for thirty minutes while treading water, it was the last straw. Or maybe it was when he crawled over my back and taunted, "You fucking love having me on top of you, don't you?" that I came unglued.

I dragged him under and kicked him in the gut. Hard. The surprise factor worked in my favor...for five seconds, anyway. As soon as it wore off, Gabe came after me in his patented subtle way. He gouged my side, then flailed to the surface and put on a show for our meager audience. He should have won an award. His dramatic gasps for air and subsequent coughing fit sent a twitter of worry through the crowd. When he swam to the edge to gather himself and catch his breath, he received a round of applause. And me? I got kicked out of the game.

I was forced to endure the last quarter from the bench in disgrace. And to add insult to injury, we lost. Everyone was pissed...my coach, my teammates. But no one was angrier than me. I shouldn't have let Gabe get under my skin. There was no excuse. I'd played this game for more than half my life. I knew better than to let an opponent inside my head.

Coach Burton pulled me aside afterward. I braced myself for a long-winded, expletive-filled verbal beatdown, knowing on some level I probably deserved it. But I had to admit—at twenty-three, this shit was getting old. I secured my towel and cocked my head, focusing on the angry vein pulsating at Coach's temple.

He was a super-fit, no-nonsense drill sergeant in his late forties with graying hair, who lived and breathed water polo. He'd won numerous accolades in his career as an athlete and a coach. I had the utmost respect for him, but I hoped he'd finish berating me sooner rather than later.

"...you better learn to control your fucking temper," he yelled, pointing a warning finger at my chest. "You're an important member of this team, Vaughn. You and Chadwick will be unbeatable together if you get your head out of your ass and—"

"Sorry, sir. Um, what do you mean by 'unbeatable together'? He plays for the enemy."

Coach Burton lifted his bushy brows and leaned in conspiratorially. "Not for long. He's coming to Long Beach."

No fucking way. I frowned and then shook my head, hoping he'd crack a smile and laugh at me for taking everything so damn seriously.

"You're kidding, right?" I prodded.

"Nope. I'm serious. And after the way he handed us our lunch, I'm fucking thrilled."

"But when...and why?"

"Next week and who cares?" he quipped. "We need Chadwick to be competitive this year. But the only way this works is if you play nice. I need you to make him your best goddamn friend. Got it, Vaughn?"

I nodded distractedly. "Got it."

Coach patted my shoulder and bellowed at someone behind me before ambling away. I let out a beleaguered sigh, then pushed away from the wall and willed myself to relax. I had one year left. It was pointless to stress about personnel changes. If I were smart, I'd concentrate on my future after graduation and remember that some things were beyond my control.

But having Gabe for a teammate was just...alarming.

THE PROBLEM with being a type A control freak was that I couldn't let anything go. I had a terrible habit of twisting and turning over minute details and sweating the small stuff. I'd lie awake at night thinking about a test I had to ace or an appointment I had to make. Timeliness and general organization mattered to me more than they did to most of my friends. Evan was a great example.

He lay sprawled on our sofa in front of the flat-screen with a bag of chips on his stomach, typing something into his phone with his left hand while he reached aimlessly for the remote on the coffee table a foot away.

"What are you doing?" I asked, picking up the remote and swiping the chips away in one fell swoop,

"Hey! I was eating those and watching that and—why are you all dressed up?" Evan furrowed his brow and sat up when I perched on the armchair next to him.

"We're going to Chelsea's party, remember? You need a shower. Hop to it." I tapped my watch obnoxiously, then busted up laughing at Evan's blank stare.

Evan di Angelo and I had been roommates since our freshman year in the dorms. He transferred to a nearby private college to play football our sophomore year, but he didn't want to deal with finding a new apartment and new roommates, so he commuted twenty minutes to school. Truthfully, the deal here was too cushy to pass up. My parents bought this bungalow two blocks from the beach because they wanted to be sure I lived in a good neighborhood. In other words, they were overprotective helicopter parents. They liked Evan and invited him to stay at the beach house free of charge. Kinda like they were bribing him to be my friend. We'd laughed about it at the time, but there was something a bit...overbearing about the offer.

"Dude, chill. I took a shower after my game. I'm exhausted. Have a beer and watch some football. We don't want to be the first ones there. Trust me," he said, giving me a dose of sideways realness.

"I guess you're right. Want another?"

"You're reading my mind. Thanks, man."

I returned with two bottles. I uncapped them both and slid one across the coffee table before reclaiming my seat.

"This game sucks," I commented, noting the twenty-four to zero score in the fourth quarter.

"Yeah, there's nothing much on. Might as tell me who got in your grill. You look pissed."

Evan's intuitive side always took me aback. He might have seemed like a typical jock, but he was surprisingly sensitive. He was six foot two, two hundred and thirty pounds with light-brown hair, brown eyes, chiseled cheekbones, and a straight nose. And he was built like a brick house. No one in their right mind would mess with Evan. Until they got to know him and realized he was a big, good-natured teddy bear who liked watching sports, hanging with his buddies, and playing video games. Other than height, we were complete opposites. I was lean and broad-shouldered with short dark-blond hair, blue eyes, and tan skin. I looked like a typical California kid, except I lacked the stereotypical easygoing attitude. I thrived on stress.

"Pissed isn't the right word. I'm..."

"Irked, befuddled, annoyed?"

I nodded in agreement. "You sound like you swallowed a thesaurus but yes, that's exactly it."

I gave Evan a brief rundown from my game that morning, highlighting key points of my underwater wrestling match with Gabe.

"Sounds like a regular day at the office. What's the big deal?"

I yanked my button-down shirt from my jeans and turned to show him the wicked-looking scratch on my side. "Look what he did to me!"

Evan gamely leaned to check out my war wound. "Poor baby. Didn't Amanda do that to you too?"

"That was different," I huffed. "This isn't a love mark in the heat of the moment. This fucking hurts!"

"Hmph. But it *was* a heat of the moment thing. Maybe Gabe swings both ways, and he's trying to let you know he wants you." Evan's faux-serious tone made me laugh.

"You're an idiot." I smacked him upside the head, then flopped back into the armchair. "But you're right. I wouldn't think twice about any of this, except Coach informed me Gabe is transferring. He's going to be my new teammate."

"Oh...the plot thickens." Evan rubbed his hands together gleefully and waggled his eyebrows. When I didn't crack a smile, he cocked his head. "C'mon, Der. You've been talking about what a kickass player Gabe is for years. And if he's occasionally kicked *your* ass, doesn't that mean he'll be a fierce teammate?"

"Maybe, but he's a dick," I groused.

"Hey, he could be a great guy outside of the pool, but who gives a shit? If you ask me, I bet you're mad no one cleared his transfer with you first. You like to be consulted on these things."

"Yeah, well..." I didn't deny it. As team captain, I would have appreciated a heads up. My anally retentive nature demanded to be in the know.

"Why's he transferring anyway? Isn't he a senior?" Evan asked, glancing back at the television distractedly.

"Yeah, but I don't know if he's staying on for another year or not. As far as why...I think he just made the national team. It's basically a pre-Olympic training squad. Their coach runs practices at a nearby pool. But that's just a guess. I have no idea." I swiped my hand through my hair, then reached for my beer.

"You can ask him tonight. I bet you twenty bucks Chelsea invited Gabe to her party."

"What? Why would she?"

"You know Chels. She loves fresh blood. If she's heard Gabe's transferring, she'll invite him. Which means...your new best buddy may be there tonight. If he is, it's a great time to shake hands and agree to be friends. And if things go well, maybe you can get him to scratch you in a way you might actually like."

"You're hysterical. Get dressed and let's grab something to eat. I'm hungry."

WE STOPPED at a bar on 2nd Street for a pre-party dinner. We chatted about sports, school, and current events over burgers, fries, and a couple of beers and then walked to Chelsea's place. It was a wise decision to leave our cars behind. There was no parking in front of her house. I had a feeling that would be the case. School started next week and summer wasn't quite over, which meant beach towns up and down the Southern California coast were bombarded, and parking spaces were hard to come by.

I paused in the doorway to get my bearings and blinked at the instant sensory overload. The lights were dim, the music was at near concert-level decibels, and the living room was a swarm of humanity. I spotted our hostess dancing on a coffee table. Chelsea Ramirez was one of my best friends and a self-proclaimed party girl. She was outgoing and friendly, and she loved hosting impromptu get-togethers for fifty or more people. Her roommates were obviously in on the fun, but we all knew Chelsea was the catalyst. Her bi-monthly parties were a staple in the five years I'd lived in Long Beach.

Chels was a pretty, petite Latina with long brown hair and a bohemian vibe that drew people to her. I glanced at the good-looking blond, blue-eyed guy dancing with her. Mitch was one of Chels's "party pals." Her words, not mine. He was one of those high-energy, life-of-the-party types. In other words, Chelsea's male equivalent. Over the past few years, he'd morphed from a shy, quiet kid to an out-and-proud member of the cheer squad and a leader in the university's Queer Alliance club. I didn't know Mitch well, but I liked him and I respected his relentless confidence.

Chelsea yelled my name, holding Mitch's arm for support when she teetered on her high-heeled boots. I couldn't hear a word she said, but I thought she was inviting me to dance. Hell, no. Not without liquid courage. I waved, then tipped my hand toward my mouth in a universal "I need a drink" gesture before greeting a couple of my teammates standing near the galley-style kitchen.

"What's that?" I yelled above the din of an old Drake song, pointing at the pink cocktail in Troy's red cup.

"No clue. It's in the punch bowl in the kitchen. It's pretty good."

"Dude. Didn't your mama ever tell you not to drink from the community party bowl? Someone could have slipped something in there," I admonished.

"Don't be a party pooper, Vaughn. At least taste it," he said, pushing his cup at my chest.

I held my hands up and shook my head. "No, thanks. I'm gonna find a beer."

I weaved through the mass of people, braving the impossibly small and very crowded space. I stopped to give a couple of high fives on my way to the keg located outside the kitchen door.

The evening air felt refreshing after the claustrophobic press of bodies inside. I sucked in a deep breath before skirting around a makeshift bar and heading for the keg. I filled my cup, then stepped into the shadows and surveyed the backyard. Two separate groups were chatting near the barbeque. Their inebriated laughter almost drowned out the telltale sounds of a couple engaged in a heavy make-out session a few feet away under a giant pepper tree. I sipped my beer and was about to head back inside just as one of the lovebirds stepped out of the shadows.

"Oh. Derek, it's you. Hi."

I couldn't see her well in the dark, but I'd recognize that voice anywhere. I pasted a smile on my face and turned to greet my ex-girlfriend and—

No fucking way.

I knit my brow and cast a wary glance between Amanda and my nemesis.

"Hey," I said awkwardly. "How's it going?"

"Good. Um...you guys know each other, right? Water polo and...stuff." Amanda pushed a strand of her long blonde hair behind her ear and bit her already swollen bottom lip.

The sudden wave of jealousy took me by surprise. I broke up with Amanda last June. We'd been together for two years and we'd had a good run, but there was no real passion between us. We'd become a habit, and I hadn't seen the point in drawing out a relationship we both knew wouldn't last. She'd seemed hurt at first but okay after a few weeks, and I'd been relieved. So I didn't understand. Why would I care if Amanda and Gabe got together? Sure, it was weird...but we were all adults. I had no right to envy, and I certainly shouldn't feel like I'd been sucker-punched. The weird thing was that my angst had nothing to with my ex. This was all about Gabe. I couldn't tell if I was upset he was with her or with anyone in general. I was too confused to touch that.

I refocused and nodded brusquely. "Yeah. We know each other."

Amanda stepped away from Gabe and shot a wan smile at both of us. "Um, I'm going to use the restroom. I'll see you guys around."

I smiled tightly and watched her walk away before turning to Gabe. He looked good tonight. He was dressed like me, in jeans and a short-sleeved button-down shirt. He was the kind of guy most people considered hot. And why the fuck did that even cross my mind? Okay, it was probably because I usually saw him in a Speedo and he always looked hot but—*oh, fuck.*

"Um, are you and Amanda...?"

"Nah. We were just...foolin' around."

"Oh. Do you make a habit of sticking your tongue down random girls' throats?" I asked in a sharper tone than I intended.

Gabe snorted. "No, but she came on to me after I asked about you and...*bam*! Before I knew what hit me, she backed me against that tree. Then you came snooping around and ruined everything."

His tone was jocular and laid-back. The polar opposite of the warrior I did battle against in the pool this morning. The personality shift was jarring. I didn't trust him at all.

"Why did you ask about me?"

"I didn't. It was a joke," he snarked.

"Oh. Right."

A Saturday that began and ended with Gabe wasn't good for my sanity. I started to turn away when he spoke again.

"Good game today."

"Better for you than me," I huffed.

He gave me a lopsided grin and shrugged. "Win some, lose some."

"So says the guy who gouged my side, then somehow convinced the ref he was the injured party."

Gabe's smile lit his eyes. I could practically feel the warmth emanating from him. It made me want to return the gesture, which didn't make sense. Gabe and I weren't friends. Hell, I'd caught him with my ex five minutes ago.

But that smile...

"I'd apologize for the teensy scratch, Vaughn, but you kicked me in the stomach one too many times. You were aiming for my nuts, and I wasn't going down without a fight. The key is to not get caught," he said with a wink. "You oughtta know that by now."

"Hmph." I sipped my beer, then slipped my free hand into my pocket so I wasn't tempted to wring his neck when I inched closer to him. "Coach told me a funny story after he chewed my ass out for getting benched. He said you were transferring and...crazier still, he said you were joining my team."

"*Your* team?"

"I'm the captain so yeah, it's my team. Is it true? It must be. Why else would you be at Chelsea's party? Did she invite you? If she did, don't get too excited. She's awesome but she'll be the first to admit, she extends random invites to hot guys."

Gabe's eyes twinkled good-naturedly. "So you think I'm hot?"

"What? Fuck you. No," I sputtered.

"Aw. I think that's super sweet. Don't worry. I won't tell anyone you like me," he teased.

"I don't."

"Maybe a little? I kinda hope so, 'cause to answer your earlier question...yes. We're gonna be teammates and probably best friends before you graduate. You are graduating, right? You've got to be twenty-five now."

"I'm twenty-three, dickhead. And yeah, I'm graduating. Why are you transferring?"

"Long story short, the national team is training in Long Beach now. I can't waste time commuting to LA for school, then back here for practices. The only way to get a degree and have a shot at the Olympics is to be in one central location."

"Oh," I said like a true lame-ass. "When are you gonna start practicing with us?"

"Next week." Gabe rubbed his hands together before offering me his right one. "Let's call truce, ol' buddy, ol' pal. What d'ya say?"

I stared at his outstretched hand for a moment and was about to shake it when someone bumped my elbow.

"This stuff is fucking awesome. Take a drink," Evan insisted, prying my beer from my fingers and replacing it with another red cup. "And don't worry, I made it myself. No funny business. Hey, Gabe. I think we've met at a water polo game or something. I'm Evan."

I sipped the cocktail while they exchanged bro-style fist bumps and introductions. "Not bad. What's in it?"

"Vodka, triple sec, vodka, lime juice, and more vodka," Evan replied proudly.

"In other words, it's a very strong kamikaze."

"Exactly. You're welcome. Give Gabe a taste. If you like it, I'll make another one," Evan said.

"No, thanks. I don't drink during the season." Gabe smiled at Evan, then turned and clasped my shoulder. "I'll see you at practice Monday...Captain."

Gabe moved away before I could respond, which was probably for the best. I'd just spent five minutes alone with him and miraculously, it wasn't horrible. In fact, he was vaguely...pleasant. Although that parting line might have been a judgment call. Like he couldn't believe the team captain would party during a crucial time. Technically, this was still pre-season. I took another drink, then handed the red cup back to Evan.

"Keep it. Look at you—making friends with the enemy. I'm proud of you, little buddy," he gushed sarcastically.

I scoffed. "We're not friends but if we're going to be teammates, I might as well make the best of it."

"Good idea. It's cool of you to make an effort. That's what counts."

"Don't give me too much credit. I didn't go looking for Gabe. I bumped into him and Amanda making out," I informed him with a world-class eye roll.

"Your Amanda?" he asked incredulously.

"She's not *my* Amanda. She's a free agent. We broke up," I reminded him as I lifted the cup to my mouth. "Damn, this is strong."

"Mmmhmm. Isn't that gonna be weird for you if your ex starts showing up at your games drooling all over the guy you hated until ten minutes ago?"

"Nah. Gabe said they aren't a thing anyway."

"I like your attitude, man. But if they aren't a thing, I think she's trying to change that."

Evan gestured toward the grassy area where a large group convened around a fire pit. Some were chatting, some were dancing. And on the fringe next to a potted plant, Gabe stood with his arm draped over Amanda's shoulder. I noted her hand dipped in his back pocket and fuck, there it was again...a stabbing pang of something that felt a lot like misdirected jealousy.

I gulped the cocktail greedily, tipping the cup back until it was empty. "Who cares? It's not my business. Make me another one? This might be your best drink yet," I enthused, moving toward the side door.

I studiously averted his gaze and tried not to care that Evan probably assumed I regretted my decision to end a perfectly fine two-year relationship. I had zero regrets. But I couldn't explain what was really going through my head when I didn't understand it myself. This visceral, possessive feeling deep inside me had nothing whatsoever to do with Amanda. It was all for Gabe.

And it freaked me the fuck out. I thought I had this bi thing under control. I hadn't looked at another guy twice in a long time. Why now? Better question...why Gabe? I couldn't begin to process my reaction, which meant...this was a job for alcohol.

TWO AND A HALF HOURS LATER, I was drunk. Toasted, bombed, schnockered. Whatever the word was for total incapacitation with a limited ability to speak coherently or walk without bumping into inanimate objects. I wasn't the only one. Some of my fellow partiers were dancing on tables; others lost key articles of clothing as they grinded against each other. And I was pretty sure I heard the telltale sounds of sex in progress when I passed the guest bedroom. Then again, I wasn't "sure" of anything. I was dazed and confused.

I cut myself off just after midnight and sat on the deck in the backyard, guzzling water while my friends debated the state of hip-hop music's cultural influence. Or maybe they were just talking about scoring tickets to Coachella next year. I had a hard time following. Thankfully, it wasn't a conversation that required much input. I was happy to hang out, stare at the stars, and be grateful Gabe had disappeared. And not with Amanda. I eyed her across the lawn, chatting with a couple of her sorority sisters and Mitch and Evan.

I'd have to ask Evan what they talked about tomorrow. But now...I just wanted to go home. I sent Evan a quick text and waited for him to respond. I watched him pick his phone from his pocket, glance at the screen, and then shove it back without replying. *Asshole.* I tried again.

Are you ready?

Evan retrieved his cell again, then shot a dirty look at me and shook his head no just as one of Amanda's friends slipped her hand under his shirt. Or maybe it was Amanda. I couldn't tell and I no longer cared. I gave a series of exaggerated hand signals to let him know I was leaving. Then I stumbled to my feet and said a round of good-byes before making my way through the house and out the front door.

I paused to uncap my water bottle on the sidewalk and noticed a figure standing in the street next to a smallish car. The contrast of the tall man and the tiny vehicle caught my attention. I couldn't tell who it was but when he waved, I returned the gesture and continued down the block.

"Hey, Vaughn! Did you hear me?"

"Huh?" I stopped in my tracks, then walked back toward the car and cast a wary gaze between the Mini Cooper and the guy I'd been avoiding for the past three hours.

"It's me...Gabe. Do you want a ride?"

Did I? My head felt clearer than it had an hour ago, but I was still tipsy. "Um..."

When I hesitated a second too long, he laughed, then moved to open the passenger-side door. "Get in. You're drunk."

I obeyed but of course, I felt the need to defend myself. "I'm not drunk."

"Yeah, you are," he countered without heat.

"Okay, maybe I'm a little drunk, but I'm not totally gone. I just feel loopy, you know?"

"I've been there. But I've been drinking water all night, so you're in good hands. Where do you live?"

"Four blocks away. I'm on Coronado. Why are you still here? I thought you would have invited my ex back to your place by now," I said conversationally, setting my empty water bottle in the cupholder before fastening my seat belt.

"You're a dick, Vaughn."

I chuckled at his beleaguered sigh and twisted in my seat to face him. God, he was so...chiseled. He reminded me of a Greek statue with his high cheekbones and strong jaw and—*oh, fuck*. I willed myself not to say anything stupid when that odd, crushy feeling came over me again. It made me feel tingly inside and reckless.

"I have my moments. But you're a bigger dick than me," I argued.

"How did you know I have a bigger dick than you?"

"Ha. Ha." I unbuckled my belt and was about to unzip my jeans when Gabe set his hand over my wrist.

"What are you doing?"

"I'm gonna prove my dick is bigger," I slurred. Yep, my hidden reckless side had resurfaced and gone rogue.

Gabe paused at the stop sign and looked over at me. "Not necessary. Put your python away, Vaughn, and tell me where to go."

I chuckled heartily. "It's four blocks up on your left. I think."

"Got it. Just so we're clear, I'm not into your ex. She seems cool, but there's nothing between us."

"Did I say there was?"

"Yeah. When you first got in my car. Are you okay?" he asked, sounding slightly concerned before adding, "Zip up those jeans. If we get pulled over, I don't want to have to explain why my passenger has his dick out."

This time, I threw my head back and laughed like a loon. "That would be hilarious. Don't worry. My dick isn't out."

"Zip up your jeans," he repeated.

"I can't. They're too tight. I'll do it when I get home. Thanks for the ride, by the way. Sorry if I was a jerk earlier," I said, adjusting myself.

I noted Gabe's double take as he homed in on my crotch. No doubt he was wondering what the hell had gotten into me. I was definitely not myself. I was known for being cool under pressure and always in control. I hardly recognized this vodka-infused version of myself, though I had to admit, it felt strangely liberating to speak my mind and—literally and figuratively let it all hang out.

Gabe refocused on the road and pursed his lips. "I never said you were a jerk."

"Oh. Okay. Well, Amanda is a great girl, and she's obviously into you. If you like her and she feels the same, I wish you well," I assured him.

Gabe scoffed sarcastically. "Gee, thanks."

"Hey! I'm trying to be cool here. You probably don't know many people at college outside of water polo, and the entire team hates you," I teased. "We'll adopt you as one of our own eventually but in the meantime, you should meet more people like Chelsea and Amanda. Chelsea especially. She knows everyone."

"That's what my mom said. She's either worried I'm gonna get mugged or worried I'll never meet anyone 'cause I never go out." He huffed in amusement as he turned onto my street. "One minute it's, 'Gabe, you need to meet kids your age' and the next, 'Gabe, watch out. They all do drugs.' I can't win. And reminding her that I'm twenty-two doesn't seem to make a difference."

I snickered at his affected falsetto, tapping the window when we approached my house. "It's the one with the big olive tree in the front. Where do your folks live?"

"Mom lives in Glendora. Dad lives in Arizona. New wife, new family. I'll see him when I graduate or if I make the Olympic team." He pulled into a parking spot in front of my neighbor's house, then turned in his seat to face me. "What about you? I've seen your parents at games. Not today, though."

"Thank God. They would have been pissed at me for winding up on the bench. Even if it was your fault," I huffed.

"Whatever you say, Der. Water polo is a rough game. You've got to give it your all, take risks, and occasionally put on a show. I'd say it was bad luck that the ref caught your jab last but the truth is, you let emotion get the better of you. You got mad, and it made you careless."

I glared at him in the darkened car and leaned across the console. In a Mini Cooper, I probably looked like I was trying to sit in his lap.

"Just when I think I could like you, you open your mouth."

"I thought we agreed to a truce."

Gabe cocked his head and gave me a wicked lopsided grin. It was slow-growing and kind of...sexy. *Fuck. Wait. No, I didn't mean that.* He wasn't sexy. 'Cause your teammate wasn't sexy; he was just another guy. My dick didn't get the memo. It swelled in my boxer briefs, making me extraordinarily glad I'd unzipped. I would have passed out otherwise.

"Hmph. It's hard to trust the guy who slashed open my side with his fingernails," I snarked without heat.

Gabe rolled his eyes. "Oh please. I may have accidentally scratched you but—"

"Scratch?" I unbuckled my seat belt, then yanked my shirt from my jeans and pulled it up over my right side, twisting to show him my wound. "Look at this."

Gabe undid his seat belt too and squinted as he turned. "Can't see a thing. You must be overreacting."

"You must be blind," I retorted. I stuffed my shirt back into my jeans and nudged my half-hard dick. *Fuck.* I had to get out of there before I embarrassed myself. I reached for the door handle and inclined my head. "Thanks for the ride. I guess I'll see you at practice next week."

"Right. Hey, do you mind if I use your bathroom before I go? I've had four bottles of water, and I'm not sure I can make it home. At least not comfortably."

"Yeah. Come on."

I led the way up the hedge-lined path to my Craftsman-style bungalow, rezipping and reassembling myself as I moved. I'd forgotten to leave the porch light on, so it took me a second to get the key in the lock. Once we were inside, I flipped the switch in the living room and directed Gabe toward the bathroom down the hall before heading for the kitchen. I grabbed a bottle of water, twisted the cap off, and guzzled half of it in record time. Then I set it on the counter and glanced around the pristine space.

My place was a two-bedroom, one-bathroom bungalow built in the 1940s. A lot of the original features were intact—like hardwood flooring, subway tiles, arched doorways, and interesting niches carved in random walls. We even had a fireplace. And the backyard was killer. A massive wood deck just off the kitchen led to a huge grassy lawn with lemon and apricot trees lining the perimeter. In other words, this wasn't a typical residence for a couple of early twentysomethings.

I leaned against the counter and finished my water. My head was beginning to clear. Of course, that was what I'd thought before I'd almost pulled my dick out of my jeans. Maybe I just needed a good night's sleep. It had been a long day. And a weird one. I could never have dreamed up a scenario featuring Gabe Chadwick in my house after this morning. But here he was.

I gave him a thorough once-over as he walked into the kitchen. And again, the first thing that crossed my mind was, "Wow, he's really fucking hot."

"Nice place."

"Thanks. Do you want some water or something?" I asked, awkwardly pointing at the fridge.

"No, thanks. I've had enough tonight," Gabe replied with a laugh.

I should have said good-bye then and escorted him to the door, but I had a strong desire to keep him talking and maybe dispel the weird admiring thoughts going through my brain. Yes,

Gabe was a good-looking guy, but I shouldn't be fixating on his long eyelashes and the way the kitchen light framed him in a halo of sorts. I couldn't let him go until my brainwaves returned to normal, and he was the same annoyingly smart and talented opponent I'd played against occasionally for years. The thing was, I didn't really know him and at that moment, I wanted to.

"Where do you live?" I asked.

"About fifteen minutes away. I scored an apartment by campus. I have one roommate. Brent's a volleyball player. We might get a third to cut expenses, but I don't want to share a room, so that'll be up to him."

"Sharing a room gets old fast. Evan and I knew we wanted to live together, but I'd probably smother him in his sleep if I had to listen to him snoring every night a few feet away from me," I said in a lame-ass effort to keep him talking.

Gabe chuckled. "That would be rough. Evan seems like a cool guy. Is he as neat as you? This house is spotless."

"No, that's all me. I can't help it. I have a thing about order. Evan's a slob. You should see his room. At least he tries in shared spaces. I don't bug him about his unmade bed, scattered clothes, and random dishes he leaves on his nightstand as long as he keeps the bathroom and kitchen tidy. He's been on the receiving end of a couple of classic Vaughn meltdowns," I said with a self-deprecating shrug.

"A Vaughn meltdown," Gabe repeated. "That must be a version of what I experienced this morning when you tried to drown me."

"Fuck off." I laughed, then looked away quickly when a rush of heat flooded my cheeks. *Oh, my God. Please don't let me blush. Not now. He'll know something's wrong.*

Gabe stepped closer and cocked his head. "Are you blushing?"

Great.

"I don't blush."

"Whatever you say. So what's a Vaughn meltdown out of the water like? Do you scream and throw shit?"

"No, I save the physical stuff for the pool. In my normal life, I tend to get passive-aggressive."

"How so?" he prodded.

"Well, last week Evan left his sneakers on the coffee table. I repeat. *On the* coffee table. That kinda pissed me off, so I threw them outside. Usually he'd laugh it off, but there was a thick marine layer the next morning, and his shoes were sopping wet when he found them. He wasn't happy."

"What did he do?"

"He hid the remote and my car keys, and he wouldn't give either back until he blasted me for my passive-aggressive asshole tendencies."

"So you call each other on your bullshit."

I chuckled. "Yeah, I guess we do."

"You're lucky. You must be good friends," he commented somewhat wistfully.

"We are. It probably helps that we don't play the same sport. I'm close to my teammates too, but Evan and Chels are my best friends."

Gabe shot a puzzled look at me. "Chelsea? You barely said two words to her tonight."

"How would you know? Were you watching me?"

He looked vaguely uncomfortable when he replied. "No, I just—"

"Well, Chels and I aren't party friends," I intercepted before I inadvertently made things awkward. "We're real-life buddies, if you know what I mean. We bonded over Thoreau in American Lit our sophomore year. We meet for coffee a couple of times a week and talk about school, family, and boring everyday things. But at parties, she's usually dancing on tables while I hang out in a corner with the other wallflowers. She's a little wild and I'm...not."

"So says the guy who's gonna wake up with a massive hangover," he teased.

I let out a half laugh. "I'll be fine. I just need some sleep. Hopefully, the gaping wound in my side won't keep me awake all night."

"Right," Gabe snorted. "Let me see it."

I pulled my shirt off and gestured at the angry red scratch above my hip. "Do I need a tetanus shot?"

He rolled his eyes, then bent to examine my side. His expression went from derisive to vaguely concerned in a heartbeat. "*I* did that?"

"Yeah. Thanks, asshole." I kept my tone light, expecting him to taunt me for being a wuss, but he seemed genuinely puzzled. Maybe even remorseful.

"Did you put any antiseptic cream on it?"

"No. I figured the chlorine would work its magic. I'm fine. I've had worse," I said with a laugh.

Gabe straightened and frowned. "Do you have any Neosporin?"

"Uh...I think so. But don't worry about it. I told you, I'm fine," I insisted.

"C'mon. I'll help you put some on. It's in a weird spot, so it might not be easy to reach on your own." He grabbed my elbow and steered me toward the bathroom.

"Gabe, I—"

"Humor me. A little Neosporin won't hurt you, and it's better to be safe than sorry anyway. Where is it?" he asked, pointing at the medicine cabinet and then the row of drawers under the bathroom sink.

I sighed heavily as I opened the medicine cabinet and pulled out the small tube of cream. Gabe plucked it out of my hand and squeezed a tiny amount onto his forefinger before instructing me to turn around.

"Really?"

"Really."

He seemed more determined than me, so I obeyed. I leaned against the counter and watched him in the mirror. He bent slightly, then smeared the cool cream along the scratch. I nearly jumped out of my skin. His touch was warm and soothing. I sucked in a breath and bit my lip when my dick twitched in immediate response. *This couldn't be happening.* I tried to think of anything and everything un-sexy to minimize the damage and hoped he didn't notice the growing bulge in my jeans inches away from his head. Family vacations, cafeteria food...fuck, it wasn't working. Desire and need tingled at the base of my spine. I didn't understand what was going on with me, and I couldn't begin to sort through my thoughts with him so close.

"Uh...thanks," I said in a strangled-sounding tone when Gabe straightened.

He recapped the tube and set it on the counter, then smiled. "It's the least I can do. Sorry about that. It must hurt."

I swallowed hard and turned to face him. The scratch didn't register anymore. My cock was the only thing that hurt at the moment. "I'm fine."

Gabe smiled sweetly. "Good."

We stared at each other in a surreal standoff of sorts. The air crackled and buzzed with carnal heat. He had to notice it too. I had no clue what was going on in his head, but I couldn't seem to get myself under control. I wanted to touch him. Just once. I wanted to feel him against me.

I catalogued his handsome features: his thick dark hair, chiseled jaw, perfect nose, those full lips...and worked like mad to rein in my impulses. When I fixated on his mouth a moment too long, I sealed my fate. My heartbeat skyrocketed and my palms went instantly damp as something bigger than me took over my body and propelled me forward. I grabbed the back of Gabe's neck and crashed my mouth over his.

And unbelievably, he didn't push me away.

Any second now, I expected him to shove me against the counter and punch me. But he didn't. Maybe he was in shock. Hell, maybe we both were. I couldn't move now that I'd come this far. I was fused to him in the best possible way, and a little voice in my head—probably the same one that encouraged me to drink unlimited kamikazes and unzip my jeans in his car—encouraged me to revel in the moment while I had the chance. So I breathed Gabe in, savoring the feel of his mouth on mine and the brush of his hair on the back of my hand and waited for him to do something...anything.

We stood with our lips frozen in an almost manic press. Then he set one hand on my waist, angled his head, and softened the connection. I closed my eyes and followed his lead. I was in awe, or maybe it was plain ol' shock. I didn't know where to go from here but oddly enough, Gabe did. He traced the seam of my mouth with the tip of his tongue. I parted my lips instinctively, and that was when he pulled away.

He sucked in a deep breath, casting his gaze frantically between my eyes and my mouth and back again.

"What are you doing?" Gabe whispered.

"I don't know."

His nostrils flared and his chest heaved. He didn't seem angry or disgusted. Just bewildered. I wasn't sure how I felt, but I had to figure out a way to laugh this off. Fast. I licked my lips and prepared my "I should have warned you I was an equal opportunity drunk" speech. Of course, I hadn't known that was the case until this very moment. I'd never lost control like this before.

"You kissed me," Gabe said in a breathy voice. His eyes were glued to my mouth now. He seemed fascinated by the lazy glide of my tongue over my bottom lip.

I cocked my head. "Did I?"

My head buzzed, and my heart sputtered out of control. I couldn't begin to guess what was going through his mind. I wondered why he hadn't bolted at the same time I wanted him to move in closer. But when he did, I thought I might pass out.

"Yeah."

"You kissed me back."

Gabe frowned and if possible, he looked more intense than ever. And then he pounced.

He captured my face in his hands and covered my mouth. There was nothing innocent about this kiss. It was rough and demanding and full of pent-up need. He pushed his tongue between my lips as he wrapped one arm around my waist and tilted his hips, so his crotch rubbed against mine. *Holy fuck.* I'd never felt anything like it. I was rock hard, and so was Gabe. And that tease of friction felt like an awakening. I groaned into the connection and widened my legs to give him more room to do whatever the hell he wanted.

Gabe broke the kiss and licked my lower lip.

"Do you like this?" he asked, grabbing my ass and bucking his hips rhythmically.

"Fuck, yes. Do it again."

He did. The sweet, seductive glide of tongues and the tease of friction below made me hungry for more. I pushed aside all attempts at cohesive thought and let my body take over. I clutched his belt loops and met him thrust for thrust. At some point in our frenzied groping, it occurred to me that this would feel even better with fewer layers between us. I unbuckled and unzipped in a rush, then pressed my boxer-clad erection against his as I sucked on his bottom lip.

"Are you sure you—"

I shook my head and backed up slightly. "No questions. This feels amazing, and I want it...if you do too."

"Yeah...I want," Gabe growled. He made quick work of his belt and zipper and pulled me close.

We hissed at the sensation. It was remarkable how much more I could feel with our jeans out of the way. I wasn't brave enough to pull our boxer briefs aside. Somewhere in my alcohol-soaked brain, that thin barrier kept me in a "drunk and curious" zone. Yeah, I knew that was weak justification, but I needed something to give me permission to let go and enjoy the incredible feel of his thick shaft riding mine.

Our frantic hump session escalated to epic proportions. It wasn't long before our boxer briefs were wet with precum. Gabe ravaged my mouth with passionate kisses, squeezing my ass and pumping his hips manically. When he slipped his fingers underneath the elastic and traced my crack, I knew I was done for.

I pulled back slightly and gazed into Gabe's eyes. "I think I'm gonna come."

"Fuck, me too," he grunted, clutching my bare ass and slamming his hips against mine one last time before falling apart.

My orgasm hit seconds later. I shook like crazy as wave after wave of pleasure rolled over me like a tsunami. We clung to each other until the trembling slowed.

And then panic set in.

The immediate jolt from euphoria to fear made me sick to my vodka-soaked stomach. I swallowed against the bile in my throat and pushed at his chest. When he stepped back, I pulled my jeans up in a rush. I winced at the feel of my jizz-covered boxer briefs, but I had a bigger mess to deal with at the moment.

"I don't know what just happened," I squeaked.

Gabe stared at me until I looked his way. Then he glanced at the box of tissue on the counter longingly. If this hadn't gotten extremely awkward in record time, I would have told him to help himself and clean up. I'd seen plenty of other guys' penises in the locker room, but I'd never...I repeat, never, seen another man's erection live and in person. I might actually have fainted after what we'd just done.

"You don't know what happened?" he repeated incredulously as he zipped his jeans.

"No. I'm not—I mean...are you? I'm...it's cool. I just—"

"Nothing," Gabe said sharply.

"Excuse me?"

"Nothing happened." His Adam's apple convulsed theatrically in his throat as he shook his head. "Nothing."

I met his eyes again and gave what I hoped passed for an apologetic look. "Gabe, I—"

"No. Don't say anything," he said in a low, raspy voice.

Tension rolled off him in waves. When he balled his hand into a fist, I braced myself for attack. My mind was spinning out of control as the feverish look in his eyes grew, and his gaze darted back to my lips.

"If you're going to punch me, could we just get it over with? The suspense is killing me," I admitted.

Gabe furrowed his brow; then the corner of his mouth lifted in a ghost of a smile. "I'm not going to punch you, Der. I—fuck. I should go."

I nodded. "Yeah. Okay. I'll see you around."

He moved to the doorway and gave me a thorough once-over. In my current messed-up state, I wanted to believe he was admiring my abs, but fuck only knew what he was really thinking. He was guarded and serious-looking, kinda like he was in the pool. I knew what to do in a game, but not now. I was lost.

"See ya."

I inclined my head and watched him disappear. I listened to his footsteps on the hardwood floors, the sound of the front door opening and then closing. And then nothing. I let out a ragged sigh and turned to face my reflection.

Oh. My. God. What the fuck did I just do?

2

A light marine layer clung to the shoreline Sunday morning. I hoped the sun would burn through within the hour, though the gray skies fit my mood better. I tugged the brim of my baseball cap as I sipped my coffee and scanned the outdoor seating area. Weekends were always busy at Savvy Bean. It was a hipster coffee bar with a cool vibe that appealed to students, artists, and young professionals.

My gaze traveled from a pink-haired girl I recognized from school to a well-dressed gay couple at a neighboring table. I noted their fingers entwining over their coffee cups and the way their knees touched under the table. They looked in sync and in love. The instant pang of longing surprised me. I didn't understand it. Long Beach had a strong LGBTQ presence; I saw same-sex couples every freaking day and never thought twice about it. Until now.

Now...everything felt different. Or maybe I was just hungover and operating in a vodka-infused fog that conjured rainbows everywhere I went. After last night, anything was possible.

I glanced up when Chelsea set her cup down and flopped into the chair across from me. "You don't look so good."

She lowered her giant round sunglasses and glared at me. "Don't mess with me, Vaughn. I should still be in bed. I'm only here because you begged me to meet you."

"I didn't beg you," I said, rolling my eyes.

Chelsea pushed her glasses into place and sat back. "No, but you said it was important. What is it?"

I stared at her chipped red nail polish and the jumble of silver and gold bands on her fingers. No one did boho chic quite like Chels. She had a talent for making thrift store finds look like haute couture. Today's floral print ensemble was a perfect example. On anyone else, it would have looked like a tablecloth doing double duty as a sundress. The Fedora and big-ass sunglasses completed the picture. Her olive skin might have been a shade paler than normal, but she rocked a hangover in style.

Way better than I did. I didn't dare check my reflection. I felt like shit. There was no need for visual confirmation. I'd lain awake most of the night, analyzing what had gone down in my bathroom with Gabe. One second I was wracked with fear and regret and the next, I had my hand on my cock as I mentally replayed what had to be the sexiest hump session I'd ever experienced. I hoped some semblance of normalcy would return in the morning. The guilt and regret would probably be there, but it would be nice to feel like myself again. Preferably the version of me that didn't make passes at a hot guy.

But the memory wouldn't fade. I hadn't wantonly rubbed against any ol' guy in the heat of the moment last night. No. That was Gabe Chadwick's cock. Gabe. My archnemesis and new teammate. The enormity of the mess I'd made hit me like a proverbial ton of bricks this morning. I'd opened my eyes, darted out of bed, and promptly vomited. Then I'd brushed my teeth ten times and texted Chelsea.

I sipped my coffee and thought about how to word my confession. I wasn't sure how much I should say, but I couldn't do this on my own and I couldn't tell Evan. He was a great guy and I trusted him with my life, but he wouldn't understand. Chelsea had a ton of gay friends. Like Mitch. Of course, I was nothing like him but—

"Derek." Chelsea waved her bejeweled hand in front of my face and snapped her fingers.

"Sorry."

"Don't apologize. Just tell me what's up."

"Well, I'm..." I bit the inside of my cheek, then leaned forward with a serious expression. "Something weird happened last night."

"You mean Rory and Jenna? OMG. I know. They were a disaster!"

"Huh?"

"Complete train wreck," she huffed. "They had sex in the bathroom and then again in my roommate's bed. Loudly."

"Oh, yeah. I think I heard them."

"Well, after their epic sex fest, they got into a huge fight. I can't believe Evan didn't tell you about it. He helped Amanda and Mitch get them separate rides home."

"Oh. I didn't see Evan after I got home last night. I passed out pretty fast," I lied.

Chelsea lifted her brows. "Really? You look like you got less sleep than me. I got four hours. You?"

"Same."

"Hmph. Well, a lot of weird things happened last night." She held up her hand and counted down the weirdness manually. "Rory and Jenna, Greg Michaels puking in my neighbor's bushes, Amanda flirting with your new teammate and then making moves on Evan."

"She did? Why? He wouldn't go out with her. Ever," I said emphatically. "Amanda doesn't even like Evan. Why would she—"

"To make you jealous. Why else? She wants you to see what you gave up."

"That's crazy."

"But true. So tell me why you dragged my ass out of bed before noon on a Sunday," Chelsea said, tapping her nails on the table.

I swallowed hard and leaned forward. It took me another few seconds to find my voice and when I did, it was weak at best. "I got kinda drunk last night and did something and..."

Damn. I couldn't say it out loud. I buried my head in my hands and stared at the scratch marks on the table and willed myself to pull it together.

Chelsea set her hand on my bicep. "Der, you're a good guy. Whatever it is, it can't be that bad. I'd offer to guess but my brain isn't functioning yet and—"

"I kissed Gabe," I blurted.

She stilled her hand and then pulled away. I immediately decided that was all I could share. I wasn't ready for anything else. Those three words took everything out of me. I looked up, hoping like hell I hadn't made a mistake trusting her with this.

Chelsea seemed like the perfect confidante. She'd become one of my best friends in college over the past four years. She was open-minded, smart, adventurous, and her interest in sports gave her an appreciation for my world, even though she'd never played water polo. And she was completely uninhibited when it came to sexuality. A few months ago, she told me a raunchy story involving sex with two girls from her Women's Studies class. Until then, I'd had zero clue she swung both ways.

Then again, I had no idea I did either. Okay, not true. I'd known I was attracted to men too. I'd just hoped it would go away.

"Gabe," she repeated incredulously, pulling her sunglasses off. "You kissed Gabe?"

"Yeah. I did," I admitted, braving a glance at her.

Chelsea's eyes widened as one corner of her mouth curled in a smile that quickly took over her whole face. She held her hand up for a high five and chortled merrily when I ripped off my glasses and glared.

"Why are you leaving me hanging?"

"Because this isn't funny. I did something I can't undo, and I have to see him at fucking practice tomorrow!" I hissed.

"All right, all right. Give me the whole scoop. I'm suddenly very happy I picked up your text message at the ass crack of dawn."

"It was nine a.m.," I corrected before launching into a brief synopsis of the scene in my bathroom a mere twelve hours ago. I only shared the kiss. The rest was mine. I couldn't talk about what I hadn't fully processed. I traced the rim of my to-go cup as I wrapped up my story with a dramatic sigh. "I don't know how I'm going to get through tomorrow."

"You're going to be fine. I admit, I'm...shocked. But I think it's totally cool," she gushed.

"How is it cool? Do you realize how awkward I've made my entire last season of water polo? I had to get this off my chest before I suffocated. I don't know what it means or if it means anything at all or—"

"Pull yourself together, Der. It just means you kissed a guy."

"Yeah, but am I gay or bi, or was I curious in the heat of a drunken moment? It might take some getting used to, and maybe I'd be fine with any scenario...but why Gabe?"

"Why not Gabe? He's dreamy," she sighed in a swoony tone before continuing. "Don't ask yourself what silly label you need now. The better question is...did you like it?"

I hesitated for a beat, then picked up my coffee and set it down again. "Yeah, I did. And he did too."

"How do you know?"

"He kissed me back."

"Did he kiss you like he meant it and enjoyed it?"

"Definitely. I just wish I knew what came next," I sighed.

"Der, look at me." Chelsea waited for me to comply, reaching for my hand and lacing our fingers together. "You didn't do anything wrong. Stop freaking out. Talk to him after practice to clear the air, but quit torturing yourself. You're both adults. Do the right thing. Get the conversation over with and see where it leaves you. You might just get a boyfriend out of all this."

"Ha. That's really funny," I snapped sarcastically.

"C'mon, it's not the end of the world. It might even be a beginning and—*oh, my God*! Amanda is gonna go bonkers," she snickered, adjusting the brim of her hat.

"Geez. Don't say a word. This doesn't go beyond this table, Chels," I said in a serious tone.

She made a "zipped" motion across her lips, then smiled. "You can trust me."

"I know. Thank you."

"Are you going to say anything to Evan?"

"No way."

Chelsea shot a puzzled look at me. "Why not? He's totally chill and he's your best friend. You can trust him. And I'm always here if you need me. In the meantime, talk to Gabe. You'll figure out the rest from there."

"You're right," I agreed before taking a healthy swig of coffee.

"Of course I am." She pursed her lips in a mischievous lopsided grin. "By the way, you guys would make a really hot couple. I'd love to be a fly on that wall."

I snorted in amusement and leaned over to pull her Fedora over eyes. Chelsea batted me away, then yanked my cap off my head as payback. I shoved my hat back on and was about to switch topics when a sudden sense of urgency came over me.

"I probably shouldn't wait." I furrowed my brow and pulled out my phone. "You know everyone, Chels. Do you have his number?"

"As a matter of fact, I scored his digits when I invited him. Lucky you." She typed a message into her cell and then winked. "Go on, Der. You got this."

THE SUN finally broke through the clouds as I made my way home along the boardwalk. I stepped aside to avoid a gaggle of bike riders and glanced at my cell again. Nothing. I'd texted Gabe at the coffee shop and foolishly expected him to be on my wavelength and agree we should get any awkwardness out of the way before tomorrow. I'd labored over the simple message as though it was the opening line in an important Comp Lit essay.

Hi Gabe. This is Derek. Call me.

I reread the message five times, then pressed Send and pushed my cell into my pocket so I wouldn't stare at the screen. An hour later, nothing. So I sent another one.

We have to talk. It's important.

Still nothing.

Okay, so he probably wasn't waiting for a message from me. First of all, he didn't know I had his number and secondly, he might actually have a fucking life. He could be in the pool or out with friends. He might even be asleep. I leaned on the railing separating the boardwalk from the sand and the Pacific Ocean and stared at his contact info, willing myself not to do anything stupid. And then of course, I did it anyway.

I pushed Call and lifted my cell to my ear. I fixated on the horizon as though I was seasick as well as hungover. Too much caffeine and too little sleep were a bad combo for my delicate stomach. The added drama didn't help.

"Hello?"

My heart slammed against my rib cage. *Oh boy. Now what?* I licked my lips and gulped.

"Oh hey. Um, it's me...Derek. I...can you talk?"

Silence.

"Yeah. What's up?"

"Uh, well...I've been thinking about last night. I didn't want to wait to—"

"What about last night?"

That stopped me.

"About what happened." I paused for a moment, then added in a deliberate tone, "In my bathroom."

"Nothing happened."

"But—"

"We're cool, Derek. There's nothing to talk about. See you at practice. Later."

Click.

He hung up on me.

Okay. Well, maybe that was a good thing. Right? He didn't want to discuss it. *Move on. Let it go. Not a big deal...so don't turn it into one.*

I slipped my cell back into my pocket and stared out to sea. I did my best to calm my erratic heartbeat and relax and be grateful Gabe was willing to erase my faux pas and start over with a clean slate in the morning. This was what I wanted too. It was a good thing.

So why did I feel like he'd just kicked me in the nuts?

MY ACTING SKILLS SUCKED, and Evan knew me far too well. I figured it wouldn't take long before he noticed I was out of sorts. Thankfully, he was preoccupied with the drama I'd missed after I'd left Chelsea's last night. Particularly the part involving my ex. I laughed it off, but he was disturbed by Amanda's sudden interest in him.

"I didn't touch her, but I couldn't escape her easily either. She was glued to me, and the weird thing was that it was for your benefit, Der. She wanted everyone there to report back to you. Watch out for that one. She's got revenge on her mind. Or reconciliation," he'd added with a shrug.

"Somehow I doubt it. I don't know what her deal was, but she was all over Gabe Chadwick earlier too."

There. I did it. I said his name and it didn't sound weird or laced with longing. Or did it? I cast a sideways glance at Evan just as he twisted to face me from his perch on the sofa with a look I couldn't quite read.

"I noticed. You won't believe this. She said she was testing a rumor."

"What kind of rumor?" I asked, suddenly aware of my heart thundering in my chest.

"She said she heard Gabe's gay."

My mouth suddenly felt like the Sahara. I licked my parched lips but kept my eyes locked on the preseason football game on the flat-screen until I found my voice again. "Where'd she hear that?"

"I didn't ask. Who cares if he is? To be honest, I think she said it so that I wouldn't think it was weird that she was flirting with two guys who happen to have you in common. Teammate, room-mate...see what I'm saying? She's after you, man. Whoa! Did you see that play?"

I held up my hand for a high five, grateful for the diversion. I didn't want to think about Amanda. She was old news, and I had a hard time believing she'd bother going out of her way to make me jealous. Then again, why would she make out with Gabe and then tell Evan that she'd heard he was gay? I didn't get it.

The whole thing confused the fuck out of me. I spent all Sunday afternoon and evening sifting through my abbreviated conversation with Gabe, analyzing and overthinking his tone while doing my best to forget how fucking good it felt to kiss him. And the memory of that whispered touch of his finger on my crack and his rigid cock pressed against mine was enough to make me dizzy with desire.

I had bigger things to worry about than Amanda.

I'd kissed a boy and I'd liked it. And now, I was obsessed.

MONDAY WAS GONNA SUCK. I was sure of it. Avoidance only worked in certain situations. I'd have to brush off my seventh-grade theater chops and act like Joe fucking Cool. Or at least like it was totally normal for a team captain to drunkenly make out with a new teammate and star player.

My low expectations proved to be a blessing. Sort of. Coach introduced Gabe to the team Monday morning, then gave us a set of drills and told us to get to work. End of discussion. Gabe nodded a brief greeting when I said hello but otherwise, he ignored me. Okay, that wasn't entirely true. He bumped my arm in the locker room after practice and gave me an awkward, hooded look before pretending to search for something in his workout bag.

"Hey. Are you okay? You were pretty drunk the other night."

"Yeah. I'm fine." My bored tone in no way matched my erratic heartbeat.

"So we're cool?" he asked, fixating on my mouth with an intensity that brought Saturday night back to mind in full color. His passionate kiss, roving hands, and his thick cock riding mine through two layers of precum-soaked cotton.

I licked my lips and looked away. "Of course," I grunted.

Gabe didn't move for a long moment. I wished I was brave enough to meet his gaze again, but I couldn't do it. Not now. I stared at his hands and swallowed hard when a strong wave of *déjà vu* immediately reminded me of how fucking amazing it felt when he squeezed my ass and grinded his shaft against mine. My instant blush probably gave me away, but thankfully he didn't comment on my splotchy skin. He nodded and then hiked his bag over his shoulder and walked out of the locker room. I breathed a sigh of relief and told myself to snap out of it, erase the memory, and restart.

But I couldn't let it go.

I thought about him nonstop. And when I wasn't daydreaming about Gabe, I researched. I read every article I could find regarding bisexuality. The definition simply stated a bisexual person was attracted to both sexes. However, further research indicated that romantic attraction and sexual attraction varied. I might not be attracted to a man and a woman in the same way, at the same time, or to the same degree. For a guy who thrived on order and routine, the concept of sexual fluidity confused the hell out of me. Was this my new identity? I'd always been into women. Sure, I'd thought some men were hot too, but I hadn't wanted to fuck them. Or maybe I had, but fear kept me from considering it a possibility. Until Gabe.

In the midst of grappling with the "new" me, I decided to test my physical attraction to men and Google some gay porn. My finger hovered over the return key for a good few minutes. My palms were slick, my forehead glistened with sweat, and my heart thumped like crazy. I wrote a disclaimer in my head in the unlikely event I had to explain the man-on-man action in my browser history. Of course, I planned to delete it but with my luck, my computer would freeze and the technician assigned to fix it would be the brother of one of my teammates. See? The anxiety was real. But I finally manned up and pushed Enter.

And holy fuck! I felt like Alice slipping into a wonderland. The vast array of options and subcategories was overwhelming. Sure, some of it was unappealing, but I felt that way about hetero porn too. After thirty minutes of mindless scrolling with my cock getting harder by the second, I gave in to temptation. I locked my door, pushed my workout shorts and boxer briefs down, and jacked off to two muscular hunks fucking on the floor in a warehouse. Suffice it to say, I didn't last long. I shivered uncontrollably when my orgasm hit just as the guy on the bottom gripped his lover's ass and begged him to come inside him. *Bam!* He might as well have been talking to me. Cum hit my chin and the keys on my laptop. I panted, then slumped in my desk chair while imaginary stars and birds circled my head. I'd clearly been missing some of the best orgasms of my life.

That meant I had to be bi. Okay, fine. I knew I was bi. I just didn't want to be. Wanting to be with a guy wasn't something I could easily explain. My parents wouldn't understand. Mom especially. I remembered the way she looked at me when she caught me staring at my cousin's boyfriend at a wedding reception when I was sixteen. Suspicious and maybe a little worried too. I'd felt the same way, and it scared the hell out of me, so I focused on my sport and only dated women. No doubt it was why I'd stayed with Amanda for so long. She was safe. And everything about being attracted to men was dangerous and messy. I didn't do well with messes. Obviously.

Admitting who I was to myself was a good first step, but I couldn't act on it. Not now, anyway. It was more important to find a way to coexist with Gabe. And ideally, not get hard every time he looked at me. That was easy enough since we did what any two guys in our situation would do; we ignored each other.

At first I was relieved. But after a couple of weeks, relief turned to annoyance. While Gabe made new friends and alliances with my guys, I silently stewed...torn between admiring his resolve and hot body and being irritated that I was the only one affected by that night.

Then one Friday morning, it all came to a head.

PRACTICE BEGAN the way it did every day. We might do ten new drills, scrimmage with local teams, spice up our routine with a run on the beach, or spend extra time in the weight room, but we always began with laps. *A lot* of laps. I didn't mind. There was nothing quite like cutting through the pool at a fast clip before sunrise. The cool water felt invigorating and in a weird way, life affirming. Like being the first to step in newly fallen snow. Five laps in, my head cleared and my thoughts evened out. I felt stronger with each turn and more focused than I'd been in weeks.

The return to calm was nice while it lasted. But the second

Coach blew his whistle, signaling the beginning of our first round of drills, my pulse jumped into overdrive. I hadn't seen Gabe yet that morning, but I knew he was a swim lane or two away. I spotted him near the net, tossing the ball with Troy. He was wearing a blue cap, number five. I dove sideways to catch an errant pass and did a double take. *Wait a second...that's my number.*

I motioned for my passing partner to hold the ball, then swam toward Gabe.

"Hey. How's it going?" I asked in a friendly tone.

"Good," he replied, keeping his gaze straight ahead. When I didn't speak or move on, he shot a sideways glance at me. "Did you need something?"

"Um. Actually, yeah...I need my cap." I gestured toward his head. Then I swam in front of him, intercepted the ball, and threw it to Troy before turning to Gabe with my hand outstretched.

He flashed a lopsided smile and shook his head. "Possession is nine-tenths of the law, Vaughn. Looks like it's mine now."

In a perfect world, I would have laughed off his insolence and pretended to understand his warped sense of humor. I might have even made the effort to find him a different cap and then brought our teammates into the discussion, publicly anointing Gabe's new number. I could have made it funny and best of all, the "welcoming" duties I'd avoided for three weeks as captain would have been complete. There were so many ways to maturely turn this to my advantage and shine as a leader.

Unfortunately, I saw red.

The haze of anger was so strong, it was impossible to think or see straight. I didn't give a fuck about the cap. I just wanted to wipe the smirk off his face. So I did what any rational person would do when he's been pushed a smidge too far. I jumped on top of Gabe and wrestled the damn cap off his head. And because he was a complete asshole, he fought back. He pulled me under and grabbed the cap from my hand, then shoved me hard. I caught his foot and yanked him with me before swimming to the surface for a gulp of fresh air. The water churned around us angrily. We probably looked like a couple of sharks battling over dinner. The crazed, frustrated energy in no way fit the crime. This was personal.

Maybe he wanted to send a message or reestablish boundaries, so I wouldn't get any ideas that he was interested in me in any capacity outside of the pool. And maybe I was pissed that he'd unearthed a side of me I wasn't equipped to deal with.

Round and round, we went in a furious circle until a loud whistle broke through the frenzy. Someone pulled us apart and dragged me to the side. I flung my arm to free myself, then sucked in a deep breath and glanced up at our irate coach standing over us with his arms crossed and a pissed-off expression on his mug.

"My office now. Both of you."

Fuck.

Five minutes later I sat, with a towel wrapped around my waist, next to Gabe while Coach Burton screamed bloody murder at me for my outrageously immature behavior. Spit flew from his mouth as he paced the length of his desk and back again like a fire and brimstone preacher at a Sunday service. And yes, his vitriol was directed primarily at me. Team captains didn't attack new members. Period. I owed Gabe and my entire squad an apology, and I owed my coach an explanation.

"What the fuck were you thinking?" Coach asked, throwing his arms in the air and glowering at me.

I bit the inside of my cheek and swallowed my pride. "I wasn't thinking. I apologize, sir."

"Apologize to Chadwick now and at your next opportunity, apologize to the team."

I bit into my cheek until I tasted blood before turning to Gabe. "I apologize."

Gabe didn't bother looking at me, which of course pissed me off even more. But I held my tongue as Coach continued.

"You can finish off practice with laps. I'm benching you for the game tomorrow too, Vaughn."

"What?" I jumped from my chair and gaped at him like a fish out of water. "You need me."

"I do, but I also need you to act like a leader. Don't argue. You'll be back on rotation next week...if you can control your temper. Oh, and one more thing. You two are about to become best friends. Starting tomorrow, you're partners in every fucking drill in that damn pool and roomies for every away tournament on the roster." Coach pointed meaningfully at the door. "Out."

My stomach turned so fast I was afraid I might vomit. I knew if I opened my mouth, there was a good chance I'd say something I'd regret. So I secured my towel around my waist as I stood and gave Coach a curt nod of acknowledgment before heading to the locker room.

My hands trembled as I fumbled with the combination on my lock. I was pretty sure I'd never been this angry in my life. The worst part was knowing I only had myself to blame. Gabe made me crazy. But I'd behaved like an ass and once again, I'd given him the upper hand. Fuck, I was an idiot. I flung open the metal locker door and shoved my towel inside. I couldn't deal with this shit now. A hundred or more laps might help. I reached for my goggles and was about to turn around when I sensed someone behind me.

"I'm sorry, Der."

I slammed the locker door, bolted the lock, and glared at Gabe. "Fuck you. You got what you wanted, you fucking coward. You want to pretend nothing happened? Fine, nothing happened. Thank you for reminding me that I hate your fucking guts."

"You don't hate me," Gabe said softly. "Look, I was just following your lead. I thought you wanted to forget about—"

"Oh, trust me, I do. Stay the hell away from me."

He moved in front of me and blocked my exit. "Hey, I didn't mean for that to happen."

"Which part? The kiss, humping in my bathroom, or pissing me off to make sure I'd get cut from another game?"

"All of it. Especially the kiss."

I furrowed my brow. "Especially? It's been a couple of weeks, but don't lie to me. I know you liked it as much as I did, and you knew exactly what you were doing."

"Of course I did." Gabe moved into my space, then cocked his head and squinted. "So you liked it."

We stood inches apart, wearing matching black Speedos and nothing else, engaged in a weird standoff I didn't quite understand. Tension rolled between us in a fierce wave that made it difficult to breathe.

"Yes. I liked it," I huffed in exasperation. "But it just occurred to me that you kissed me *and* my ex that night. Did you do that on purpose? Is this some fucked up game where you—"

Gabe pounced so fast, my head almost hit the wall. He pulled me against him before my shoulder hit my locker and then crashed his mouth over mine.

This wasn't a kiss. It was an angry fusion meant to establish dominance and control. And yeah, to shut me up. I didn't push him away. But I didn't back down either. I grabbed his face, tilted my chin, and thrust my tongue into his mouth. We groaned in unison as our chests collided. His skin was cool to the touch. I wouldn't have thought I'd want to be any closer, but the second Gabe moved his hand to my ass and molded himself against me, I changed my mind. And when he softened the pressure on my lips and glided his tongue alongside mine, the manic power play became a passionate kiss.

We made out, lost in a sensual tangle of roving hands and hungry kisses, completely oblivious to our surroundings. And that alone was madness. We were in a fucking locker room. If anyone walked in on us, we'd have a hard time explaining ourselves.

Gabe set his hand on the locker behind me and broke for air.

He bit his lower lip, casting his gaze from my mouth to my eyes before taking a cursory glance toward the door. The coast was clear. I huffed a half laugh when he adjusted his dick in his Speedo, then collapsed on the metal bench across from my locker. He braced his elbows on his knees and gestured at my crotch.

The skimpy fabric left nothing to the imagination. It hugged my shaft lovingly and forced the tip of my cock to the edge of the elastic. I reopened my locker and pulled out my towel again before turning back to him with an expectant look.

"We have to talk," I said in a small voice, wrapping my towel around my waist.

He nodded. "Yeah, but not here."

"I know."

Gabe raked his fingers through his wet hair, then flashed an amused grin at me. "That was stupid. But...it was hot."

"Would you classify that as a kiss, or is there another word for it?"

"It was a kiss, smartass," he huffed.

"Hmm. And is that like a rage thing for you?"

"What's a 'rage thing'?"

"Something you do when you get mad to blow off steam. You know, like go for a run, lift weights, kiss people..."

Gabe snorted as he stood. "I've never done that before in my life."

"You've never kissed a guy?"

"No, I've—I've done that, but...let's talk later. I don't want to do this here. I have another practice with the national team this afternoon. I can meet you after for dinner or something if you're free," he suggested.

"Like a date?" I asked sarcastically.

Gabe raised one brow. "If that's what you want."

I sensed a challenge there and I wanted to meet him toe-to-toe, but I was confused as hell. I had no idea what I'd walked into.

"I don't understand what's happening here. Fuck, I'm not even sure I like you and—"

"You like me." He gave me a lopsided smile that did funny things to my pulse, then added, "I like you too, Der. I'll text you later."

I watched Gabe walk away, in a daze. In less than a month, he'd turned my life inside out and upside down. He'd invaded my personal space in every possible way and left me feeling unsettled, unsure, and afraid. I had no idea what I'd do if the pieces of myself I'd hidden so well came tumbling out of the closet. I might lose everything. But the momentum had already shifted. There was no going back.

3

The rest of the day passed in a blur. I made my apologies after practice to my team and Gabe, then issued a warmish welcome to him before hightailing it home. I didn't want another run-in with Coach, and I didn't want to discuss my tirade with my friends. I wanted peace and quiet and an afternoon to myself. I cleaned the kitchen and bathroom and then mowed the lawn. I was about to go running when the text I'd been checking my phone for every fifteen minutes finally came through.

Hi Derek, can you meet at Habana at 7 tonight?

I stared at my cell and contemplated text etiquette with a guy I'd kissed. Twice. If Gabe were one of my friends, I'd respond immediately so I wouldn't forget. But he wasn't my friend. Not really. I had no previous experience to draw from when it came to striking the right balance of sexual interest with someone of the same sex. If I returned his message right away I might seem desperate, like I'd been sitting around waiting for him to call me all afternoon. Which was true, but still...I tried to think about what I'd do if he were a girl, but it didn't work. The mind-set was all wrong.

I set my phone on the kitchen counter and headed to my bedroom to change my clothes and find my running shoes. That would kill roughly ten minutes. Perfect. I toed off my Vans, stepped out of my khaki shorts, and lifted my T-shirt over my head just as the front door opened. I shouted a quick greeting to Evan when he called my name and finished getting dressed.

"How's it go—what are you doing?"

I frowned as I moved into the kitchen and found Evan bent over my cell, reading an incoming message.

He glanced up at me with a raised his brow. "You're popular."

I snapped my phone from the counter and shot an irritated glare at him. "Why are you reading my texts, asshole?"

Evan put his hands up in surrender and shook his head. "I'm innocent! I swear, I was just standing here and then *kapow*...your cell lit up. Don't get excited, man. They're all from Gabe. You guys are awfully chummy all of a sudden. I thought you hated him."

"He's fine. And like it or not, I have to be friendly."

"Looks like you're *real* friendly," Evan teased, waggling his brows. He dumped his workout bag on the floor, then headed for the refrigerator.

I gulped before working up the courage to scroll through my new messages.

If you want to go somewhere else that's cool
We can meet later too
The Grill on 2nd is good

Okay. A lot of messages but they were harmless. I typed a quick reply. *See you at Habana at 7.* Then I slipped my phone into my pocket, grabbed a water bottle, and tilted my chin toward Evan.

"We're 'regular' friendly. No big deal. Where've you been?" I asked, hoping to deflect attention from myself.

Evan pulled a takeout box from the fridge and gave me the "What the fuck?" look I deserved. It was a stupid question. Evan was a creature of habit and a chronic oversharer. He gave me a breakdown of his schedule every evening, whether or not I asked. He had a way of making boring information sound conversational. "I've got practice till three, then some studying to do. Want to grab dinner after?" That kind of thing. However, even if I'd forgotten his rundown from the night before, he'd obviously been at football practice. He rocked his usual "showered but fresh off the field" look: damp hair, fatigued expression, and a voracious appetite.

I uncapped a water bottle and clandestinely observed Evan shoveling leftover Chinese food into his mouth. If I was gay or bi, wouldn't I think he was at least a little sexy? By anyone's standards, Evan was a good-looking dude. He had an all-American athletic vibe reminiscent of Abercrombie ads. Square jaw, broad shoulders, toned muscles. His biceps bulged and flexed as he lifted the fork and took a giant bite of cold chow mein. Nope. I loved Evan like a brother, but I wasn't attracted to him. At all. And when he chewed his food like a cow and opened his mouth to gross me out, I knew without a doubt there was zero danger of suddenly lusting after my roommate.

"Practice," he replied, stabbing at the noodles greedily. "It was so fucking hot out there today. I couldn't wait to be done. I'm gonna crash for a couple of hours, and then I'm heading out for drinks with some of the guys. Wanna join us after your date with Gabe?"

"You're hilarious," I snorted. I flung the bottle cap at his head, then filled him in on my blowup in the pool. I finished up with a nonchalant, "We're just trying to do the right thing and get back on track as teammates, ya know?"

Evan narrowed his eyes suspiciously. "Seems like a waste of time."

"I told Coach I'd play nice, and that's what I'm doing," I said flippantly.

"Whatever. Come by afterward."

"Where are you going?"

"I don't know. I'll text you. We'll try to keep it close to Habana. You and Gabe can swing by after your powwow. Unless, of course, you want some 'alone time' with your new buddy."

Evan winked, then changed the topic to a new play they'd worked on at practice that afternoon. I did my best to act enthralled by his coach's strategic genius, but my mind was buzzing again. The last thing I wanted to worry about was running into my friends tonight. Or maybe that was silly. It wasn't like I was going to kiss Gabe in public. But kissing him in private sounded kind of amazing.

HABANA WAS a newish Cuban restaurant located a block from the ocean. Its corner lot prime location, rooftop deck, and regular live music made it an instant sensation with locals and tourists. It was always packed. Especially on the weekends. I straightened the collar on my blue button-down shirt and snuck a quick peek at my reflection in the mirrored wall next to the reception desk. I'd taken extra care getting ready tonight. The shirt was new, the designer jeans were my favorite, and my hair was on point. I might have been clueless about what came next, but I'd felt compelled to look my best. I wasn't sure why, though. This was a platonic meeting, not a date.

The hostess directed me to a semi-private booth in the back of the restaurant. Gabe looked up as we approached, and I swore my heart did a backflip against my rib cage. Holy fuck, he was hot. His dark hair looked thicker out of the pool, and the black oxford shirt he wore hugged his broad shoulders and somehow made his hazel eyes pop.

I licked my lips nervously as I slid into the leather bench across from him.

"Hey."

"Hi. You look nice," he said with a smile.

"Me? Uh...thanks," I sputtered. I was painfully grateful when the waiter came to introduce himself and take our drink orders.

Gabe motioned for me to go first before addressing the waiter in Spanish. My collective six years of the language between high school and college were enough to give me the gist of their brief conversation. He'd ordered bread and empanadas and asked for mango salsa.

When the older gentleman walked away, Gabe tapped his water glass against mine and smiled. "Cheers."

"Cheers." I sipped my water, then pushed it aside and propped my elbows on the table. "Are you Spanish?"

"Half Mexican on my mom's side. I grew up speaking Spanglish. I still do," he said with a laugh.

"Give me an example."

"Okay. *Te ves bien. Es esa* new shirt?"

I chuckled. "*Sí.* It is."

"Ha. You're a natural. I like that shirt, by the way. Your eyes look bluer or something."

His timbre was low and sexy. And when his gaze sharpened with appreciation, it took me a moment to snap out of it.

"Thank you."

Our waiter returned with my sangria and asked if we were ready to order our main course. I studied Gabe carefully, admiring his olive skin and the graceful cut of his jawline. I tuned out his words and listened to the cadence of his deep voice. It moved through me like honey.

"Do you know what you want?" he asked, ripping me from my reverie.

"Uh..." I glanced down at the menu and immediately gave up. There were too many choices. "What are you having?"

Gabe gave me a mischievous grin. "Do you trust me?"

"No. Not really."

He glowered playfully. "Trust me this time. I promise you won't be sorry."

He snatched the menu from my fingers and handed it to our waiter with instructions to "Make that two." I huffed in amusement as I plucked a piece of orange from my sangria.

"It doesn't really matter. I'm too nervous to eat anyway," I commented ruefully.

"Why are you nervous?"

"Because whatever this is"—I gestured between us before continuing—"I've never done it before. And other than the night of Chelsea's party, the only time we've ever spent together has been in the pool. And most of that time, I haven't liked you."

"Ouch. We're trying to be friends, Der. This is just dinner."

I frowned at his oversimplification. "It feels like a date. I know it's not, but—"

"It can be, if we want it to be."

"I don't know what to say to that. This is really confusing for me. For the record, I don't usually dress up for dinner with my friends, and I've *never* kissed any guy on the lips."

Gabe gave me a mischievous look as he leaned forward. "We did more than that, Der."

"Yeah, but...it didn't mean anything," I said before adding, "Do you do that all the time?"

"What? Kiss my teammates?" he quipped.

"Yeah." I nodded, then sipped my sangria.

"Never. And I can honestly say, I haven't come in my underwear in years. You were on fire."

"I was drunk. *You* have no excuse."

"I don't need an excuse, and I'm not sorry. It was hot." Gabe paused when a server set the bread and empanadas on our table and then refilled his water. When we were alone again, he continued. "Jesus, I'm getting a boner just thinking about it. Are you? Be honest."

That had to be a rhetorical question. I was so fucking horny it hurt to sit still. My dick nudged my zipper, practically begging for release. And once again, I didn't understand my reaction to him. It was madness.

I clandestinely flattened my palm over my crotch and shifted in my seat before nodding. "Yeah."

Gabe leaned with his elbows on the table gave me a cocky grin. "Yeah, what?"

"I'm not gonna say it out loud," I informed him primly.

"Tough customer. Okay, let's try something else. On a scale from one to ten, how hard are you right now?"

I gave a half laugh and looked away for a moment, then flashed a bashful grin at him. "Six."

"Liar. I'm at seven and a half right now," he reported proudly.

I chuckled at his pained expression. "Fine. Maybe I am too, but I'm also confused," I admitted. "Are you gay?"

He pulled a piece of bread apart and inclined his head. "Technically, I'm bi," he replied in a matter-of-fact tone. "I'm guessing you are too, right?"

I opened my mouth, but nothing came out. I took another drink, then swallowed hard and tried again. "A couple of weeks ago I would have said no, but I was lying to myself. The truth is... y-yeah, I am."

"Maybe you were just curious," he offered.

"Maybe. But, it's never been like that before. I mean, I've been attracted to other guys in the past, but I've never acted on it. Not like that." I pursed my lips before continuing. "I want to blame the whole thing on alcohol, but it's always been there. I just never lost control until you."

He regarded me for a moment. His expression was kind and understanding. Then a roguish smile lit his eyes, making him look impossibly handsome. "So you *do* like me."

"That might be an overstatement," I retorted.

"Fine. You're hot for me. That might actually be better." Gabe squeezed my hand impulsively, then pushed an empanada onto my plate and spooned some mango salsa to the side. "Eat something. These are delicious, especially with the salsa."

"Thanks." I smiled in amusement at the chivalrous though slightly overattentive gesture as I cut into the savory appetizer. I was tempted to refute the "hot for me" comment but I didn't see the point in denying it. The desire to climb over the table, push him flat on the booth, and grind against him was stronger than ever. I cleared my throat and refocused. *Food. I could talk food.*

"Do you like mangos?"

"Not usually. They're too sweet. But I like the salsa with this dish. Take a bite."

I narrowed my eyes at his bossy tone but obeyed. "Mmm. It's good."

"I told you so."

His boyish grin did things to me. I felt dizzy and a little in awe of him. It seemed so strange to be here, sharing a meal and talking about mangos after what we'd done. And—*oh, yeah.*

"Why did you kiss Amanda at that party?"

He shrugged nonchalantly. "She wanted your attention, and I guess I did too."

I frowned. "That makes no sense."

"Sure it does. You're too polite outside of the pool, and I'm too careful. Usually. You make me act weird."

"How so?"

Gabe shrugged. "You know, just...out of character. Want to know a secret? I wouldn't have gone to that party if I hadn't known you'd be there. Which is funny 'cause I planned to ignore you that night the way I knew you'd ignore me."

"That doesn't make any sense," I repeated, taking another bite of empanada.

"I know. Story of my life. I've never been able to say what I think on the first try. I act out and eventually have to double back and explain myself. Look, I figured I'd see you in your element, go home, and jerk off to how hot you looked in those tight jeans."

My face heated instantly. "Me? Really?"

"Hell, yeah. I've had a small crush on you for years. News flash...it exploded into an epic one, and I've been kinda miserable since you started ignoring me again."

"Oh." My jaw dropped. I had no clue he'd ever thought twice about me.

"It's true." Gabe waved his hand as though his gigantic revelation was no big deal, then continued. "When Amanda came on to me, I knew she wanted to make you jealous. That's what I meant about acting stupid. I shouldn't have kissed her at all, but I took a chance that you might notice me...and you did, so I'm not sorry," he said emphatically. "The only problem was that you were drunk. In my experience, sex and excess alcohol go hand in hand with a fuckton of regret. Especially for a straight guy who wakes up next to another dude for the first time. I was giving you an out."

"I didn't want an out, asshole. I wanted to talk to you. And I didn't wake up next to you," I reminded him.

"Did you want to?"

"No way! Of course not."

Gabe frowned. "Honestly, I get it. But that's why I didn't want to talk to you. Admit it, you probably puked in the morning and spent the rest of the day wondering how this was gonna go down. Didn't you?"

"Yeah, I did. But in my defense, I had a lot to drink and...I was scared."

"Me too."

We held eye contact for a long moment letting a thread of understanding weave into something new we might be able to share.

I nudged his knee playfully and grinned. "You stole my cap on purpose. You knew that would piss me off and—you wanted my attention again, huh?"

"Well...maybe." Gabe acknowledged with a sheepish shrug. "I had no idea you'd be such a fucking hothead," he snorted.

"I'm not, usually. Most of the time I'm very sane," I assured him. "I was so pissed when I walked out of Coach's office. I couldn't help thinking you set me up."

Gabe cocked his head in confusion. "What do you mean? How?"

"I figured you took my cap to warn me off. You probably didn't count on me going nuts, but it worked to your advantage. You'll be in the pool with the guys I've trained with for four years while I watch from the sidelines and worry you'll tell everyone what I did and—"

"I would never do that, Derek." Gabe shook his head adamantly. "I stole your cap to get your attention because like it or not, we're on the same team. Ignoring each other isn't a long-term strategy."

"And this is?" I gestured between us meaningfully.

Gabe's nostrils flared, and his eyes lit with a heated, lusty look I recognized well. "Probably not but...I want you."

I swallowed hard and bit my bottom lip. "I don't know how to do this, Gabe. I don't even know what I want."

"You're here. That's a start."

We stared at each other, lost in a sensual haze that seemed to separate us from the rest of the world.

The timely arrival of our dinner broke the spell. I wiped my damp palms on my jeans while Gabe assured the waiter everything looked great. I glanced down at the skillet in front of me filled with chicken and vegetables and a generous side of rice, beans, and plantains.

"It looks delicious," I commented, picking up my fork.

"*Fricasé de pollo*. Basically, it's a stew. I love it. My mom makes this."

"Mmm. It's good. Isn't this a Cuban dish? I thought you said you're half Mexican," I said before taking another bite.

Gabe rolled his eyes. "I am. She makes apple pie and mac and cheese too. Not just Mexican food. And this isn't necessarily a Cuban dish. I think it's a Caribbean thing. I have a Puerto Rican friend who makes a mean *fricasé de pollo*. I told my mom about it, and she decided to give it a try. She's an amazing cook."

"Did she teach you?"

"No. I get by okay. I keep it super basic. Protein shakes and veggies and pasta. What about you?"

"I'm pretty good in the kitchen. It's the one room in our house that my parents didn't use, so I had free rein to concoct experiments and learn new recipes. Our housekeeper taught me a little. The rest I've learned on my own. In my perfect world, I would have gone to culinary school."

"Go after you graduate."

"My folks are never going to be on board with that. I've taken a few hospitality courses but as far as they're concerned, that's just for fun. Real money is in business."

"Where does water polo fit in?"

"Team building, discipline, fitness. I've been playing since I was nine years old. They signed me up for water polo at our club without asking me. I thought I'd hate it. I love the water, but I just wanted to swim. Not have people yanking at my trunks and kicking my side to get the ball away from me. I liked it better than I thought I would. And then I loved it because I was good at it and it was mine."

"Like the kitchen?"

"Exactly." I grinned. "My mom plays tennis. Dad golfs. Neither of them knows anything about my sport. They probably didn't think I'd play water polo in college. I'm sure they'll be relieved when this season is over, and I finally graduate and get a job. They're totally supportive. But in a controlling way, if that makes sense. I guess it comes with being an only child."

Gabe nodded thoughtfully. "I'm an 'only' too. Different story but I get it. My dad played in college. He wanted to make me into his 'mini me.' I was doing drills with him in the pool at the local high school when I was in first grade. I hated it back then. After awhile he gave up on me, divorced my mom, and started over again. That's when I really got interested in the sport."

"Did you think he'd come back?" I asked gently.

"Maybe. I dunno." Gabe sighed and made a funny face. "Okay, yes. I was pretty sure it was my fault he left in the first place. So I made it my mission to be the best damn water polo player I could be. It didn't work. He never came back. But he claims he's proud of me. He actually called to congratulate me when I made the national team. He rarely comes to my games. He says he's busy with work, his new family, and blah, blah, blah, but I think he's holding out to see if I actually make the Olympic team."

"No offense, but he sounds like a jerk," I huffed indignantly on his behalf.

"He's a narcissist. If it's not about him, he's not interested. He liked that my mom's English wasn't great when they met. It meant she needed him. And he liked that I was a strong swimmer and a fast learner at an early age. But he didn't like it when Mom's English got better or when I voiced my own opinions. Maybe his new family is more cooperative," Gabe said with faux nonchalance.

"How many stepsiblings do you have?"

"Two stepbrothers. They're eight and ten. I can't remember the last time I saw them. Or my dad. Oh, wait. I remember now." Gabe snorted, then shook his head in disbelief. "He came to one of my games six months ago. It was a nail-biter. Double overtime turned into a shootout and thankfully we won. He offered to take me out to dinner afterward and I kid you not, he spent the entire hour giving me tips on how to improve my shot. He picked apart my game like a sports analyst. I kept trying to change the topic, but he wouldn't take the hint. Crazy thing is...we have nothing else to talk about. He doesn't know me. He doesn't know my favorite band or TV show, and I'd bet you a million bucks he has no idea what my major is."

I set my fork down and straightened my leg under the table, nudging his knee again and resting my calf against his. It wasn't a stealthy or particularly sexy maneuver, but it was the best I could do. And maybe Gabe understood. He smiled and held my gaze. When I noticed his eyes slip to my mouth, I bit my lower lip and started babbling.

"Okay...I'm curious. Who's your favorite band? What's your favorite TV show? What's your major, and what are you going to do after you graduate?"

Gabe chuckled. "Uh, let's see...Kings of Leon are cool, but I like older groups like Queen and Led Zeppelin too."

"Same here. I like all those bands. And alt-J. They're awesome."

Gabe nodded in agreement. "Favorite show...*Walking Dead*. You?"

"*Game of Thrones*."

"I've never seen a single episode," he admitted sheepishly.

"What? How can that be?" I gasped theatrically.

"Don't take it so hard, Der. It's a fucking TV show."

I smacked my palm against my forehead and slumped in the booth. "This is why we've never gotten along. We can't agree on anything important."

Gabe chuckled. "We just don't know each other outside of the pool. We can change that."

"How? What comes next?" I asked in a quiet voice.

He paused with his fork in midair and gave me a shy smile. He seemed nervous suddenly and for some reason, that leveled the playing field. It was good to know I wasn't the only one feeling oddly vulnerable.

"I don't know. We'll figure it out. Maybe we start by hanging out together a little bit."

My heart skipped a beat. I nodded but didn't speak for a

couple of seconds. "We can do that. Coach basically said we had to, so no one will think it's weird. We're teammates."

"If anything, they'll be relieved you don't want to kick my ass twenty-four seven."

"Who says that part would change?" I griped good-naturedly.

Gabe's eyes lit with ready humor and something like a carnal challenge. "I'm gonna make you like me, Der."

"I *do* like you," I croaked.

"You're gonna like me more," he said huskily.

Gabe's lopsided grin did things to me. Yes, he was good-looking and fit, but there was something special in that extra spark in his eyes. He was devilishly charming and self-assured, but he was complex and confusing as hell. All I knew was, there was much more beneath the surface than I imagined.

We talked about shows we'd loved as kids, which morphed into a chat about cartoons, comics, and Pokémon collections. I laughed aloud when Gabe went into explicit detail about how to properly care for Pokémon cards. His boyish side was endearing and unexpected.

"...label the plastic sleeves. Only one card per sleeve. If you double up, you miss the info on the back," he commented. He fumbled for his wallet and handed his credit card to our waiter before I could protest. When I was going to argue, he shook his head. "Leave it alone, Der."

"Okay. Thank you. I'll get it next time."

"Or you can cook something," he suggested.

I smiled, then dabbed the corner of my mouth to keep it from spreading into a megawatt grin. "Sure. What would you like?"

"Spaghetti," he replied immediately.

"Really? Don't you want to think about it?"

"Nope. Spaghetti is my favorite."

"All right. I'll trade you spaghetti for at least three episodes of *Game of Thrones*."

"Deal."

Butterflies fluttered in my stomach wildly, making it hard to breathe. So I reacted the way any average guy in a panic situation would....I kicked him under the table. Gabe chuckled and of course retaliated. Then he grabbed my wrist and gave me a stern look before linking his pinkie finger with mine. I had *déjà vu* of the gay couple I'd seen at the coffee shop the morning after Chelsea's party. I'd clandestinely observed them, feeling anxious yet curious. I recognized something special between them that I'd never had with a partner. Maybe I'd been looking in the wrong place all along. Maybe this was where I was supposed to be. When the butterflies went into overdrive, I felt flush and funny inside, but fuck, I felt good too.

SOMETHING HAPPENED AFTER THAT "DATE." We didn't suddenly become friends or lovers. We were just two guys who were intensely aware of each other and did our best to act normal. We avoided any unnecessary chatter in the pool or locker room, and we didn't hang out at school. But we started texting and talking in our free time. Silly conversations that had no rhyme or reason.

You gotta stop passing the ball to Michaelson until he's set, I typed. *His corner shot is off.*

Blow me. Did you see Fast and Furious?

Which one? There're a million.

Lengthy texts usually led to impromptu meetings. We'd end up sitting across from each other in a coffee shop talking for hours and finding funny ways to touch. Knees under the table, hands resting on coffee cups. It was almost innocent. Except for the part where I imagined him naked against me. I wanted to do what we'd done in the bathroom. Times ten. And the way Gabe looked at me when no one else was around made it clear he felt the same. If he wasn't going to make a move, it was up to me to let him know I wanted more.

Two weeks after our dinner at Habana, I asked him if he felt like grabbing something to eat after our game. I made a lame comment about reciprocating, when it would have been more accurate to say, "I want to talk to you for hours at a candlelit table in a semi-dark corner. And I want you to come home with me." I wasn't ready for brutal honesty, but I hoped he'd get the gist.

WE ENDED up at a very *un*fancy burger joint near the pier. I had to give up the reservations I'd made at the steakhouse nearby when our game went into overtime. It didn't matter. The idea of candlelight and a romantic overture was nice but as we chomped on fries and dissected the best and worst parts of our game, I couldn't help thinking this was better. Free-flowing repartee without uncomfortable expectation was better than sitting around with a belly full of butterflies.

By the time we stepped outside, our conversation had drifted to our favorite blockbuster summer movies.

"I'm easy. I'll watch anything, but I like the ones that don't take themselves too seriously, like *Guardians of the Galaxy*." I glanced up and down the busy street. "Did you park or valet your car?"

Gabe let out a half laugh. "I'm a poor college student, Der. I never valet. I'm on the next block."

"Okay. Um...I had Evan drop me off after I went home to shower and..." I winced and willed myself to shut up. Then I scratched the back of my neck and narrowed my eyes, hoping I'd get this next part right. I was about to leap off a cliff without a parachute so frankly, anything was possible. "We can say goodbye here or...you can come over and...I don't know...watch a movie or something. I'm not sure what—"

"Yes."

Gabe grabbed my wrist for a moment as though he was going to pull me against him. He let go immediately and shoved his hands into his pockets instead but kept his eyes locked on my lips. And suddenly I knew exactly what he was thinking. I wished he could say it or better yet, just do it. Then again, I wasn't sure how I'd react if he kissed me on a crowded street. I wasn't ready for a public display, but I was definitely ready for something more.

"Good. Evan said he's going out tonight. I'll check in with him to be sure." I pulled out my cell and attempted to walk and text at the same time.

"It's fine either way, Der. We can just hang out. We don't have to do anything," he said as he opened the driver-side door of his gray Mini Cooper.

I slipped into the passenger seat and then twisted to face him. "I want to."

He turned the engine on and then froze with both hands on the wheel before glancing at me. "You do?"

"Yeah. My palms are clammy. Either the anticipation is killing me, or this is my new normal around you. I can't tell if it's because I'm nervous about what we've already done or if I want to do it again. Maybe it's just being with you. I don't know. And I can't stop talking. So say something. Make me stop."

Gabe reached across the console and laced his fingers through mine and squeezed. "If it makes you feel any better, I'm in the same state."

"California?"

Gabe released my hand and shook his head in mock chagrin. "That was bad, Vaughn. Real bad."

I chuckled at his deadpan delivery and melted into the seat. "See? I told you I'm a mess."

An old Coldplay song serenaded us as Gabe navigated his car through the busy beach traffic. It was soothing but sexy. At that moment, I would have happily driven all night long and gone wherever he led. I just wanted to be with him.

Gabe pulled up in front of my house a couple of minutes later. Then he followed me along the pathway and waited patiently while I fumbled with the lock. I headed for the living area and pointed at the flat-screen on the far wall above the fireplace.

"Wanna watch something? Evan texted me back. He won't be home for a while. We can watch whatever you want," I blabbered. "You can choose. I'm easy."

"Good to know," he teased. When I didn't crack a smile, he set his thumb under my chin and scratched me, like a cat. "Relax, Der. It's okay."

I nodded, fixating on his mouth before lowering my gaze to his chest and his trim waist. I was aware of him giving me the same thorough once-over. I didn't know what he saw, but I liked the hungry look in his eyes. It was evidence if I needed it that he meant what he'd said. Whatever this was, we were in it together.

I sat next to him on a corner of the sectional and reached for the remote. I scrolled through adventure flicks and comedies, reading the selections aloud in a feeble attempt to refocus and get my pulse under control. Gabe weighed in occasionally, but he didn't seem to care what we watched any more than I did. We settled on *Jurassic Park*. I had no clue which number it was in the series. Hell, it could have been another movie starring a slew of dinosaurs. My concentration was shot. My senses were buzzing with awareness for Gabe. Tyrannosaurus Rex didn't stand a chance.

"Do you want anything to drink?" I whispered.

"No, thanks. Why are you whispering?"

"I don't know." I swiped my hands on my jeans and then crossed my arms and uncrossed them. "I think I need water. I'll be right back."

Gabe hooked his fingers through my belt loop when I stood and yanked me backward, so I landed almost on top of him. I scooted back a few inches and licked my bottom lip, noting his hungry stare with a satisfaction that felt foreign to me.

He lifted his fingers and tentatively traced my jawline while his eyes roamed over my face, taking inventory or memorizing my features. He placed his hand over my throat in a proprietary grip that was borderline possessive before cupping the back of my neck and leaning in to brush his nose across my cheek. My heart slammed against my chest when he rested his forehead against mine.

"Are you breathing?"

"No."

Gabe smiled. "Don't pass out."

"I'll try not to. I—are you gonna kiss me?"

"Do you want me to?"

"I think so," I replied in a raspy tone.

"I can't kiss you if you aren't sure."

His words were laced with the perfect amount of humor. I let out a half chuckle and nodded. "I think I'm sure."

He tsked and shook his head. "Not good enough. You have to be one hundred percent, absolutely, positi—"

I grabbed Gabe's face and crashed my mouth over his. He grunted in response but recovered quickly, threading his fingers through my hair. I licked his lips in a wordless request for entry, then glided my tongue alongside his. He moaned into the connection, angling his head as he gripped my shoulders before pulling me on top of him. I didn't break stride. I twisted my tongue with his, pausing to nibble his lips before capturing his mouth again.

He felt amazing underneath me. This was new in every way possible. He was taller than me with a slightly thicker build. I'd never been chest to chest, draped over another man, or had strong arms wrap around me, holding me close. But I liked it. I ran one hand along his side and arched my back, accidentally rubbing my jean-clad erection against his.

I broke the kiss and sucked in a gulp of fresh air. "Fuck, that feels good."

"It feels better without the jeans," he purred, biting my chin playfully.

I scrambled off him and held out my hand. "Come with me."

We hurried down the short hallway to my bedroom, closed the door, and came together like a couple of magnets. I set my arms over Gabe's shoulders and walked him backward until he hit the mattress. He kissed me frantically with his hands splayed on my ass. My breath hitched when he tilted his hips and rocked his pelvis against mine.

Gabe didn't pause to ask if I liked it this time. He knew. He unbuttoned my shirt and then pulled the fabric from my jeans. I did the same for him. I tried, anyway. My hands were shaking like crazy. I'd never wanted anything or anyone as much as I wanted him. And when he rolled my nipples between his thumb and forefinger while he tongue-fucked my mouth, need and desire became a fiery, visceral thing. I didn't just want him. I had to have him.

I pushed the red-and-blue striped duvet to the end of my queen-sized bed before shrugging my shirt off my shoulders. I automatically reached for my belt buckle but stopped to give him a searching look.

"Is this okay?" I asked.

"Fuck, yeah," Gabe choked.

He pulled at my belt loop and batted my hands away, expertly threading the leather before unbuttoning my jeans. He paused to stare into my eyes, with his fingers on my zipper.

"Don't stop. Please."

Gabe slowly lowered my zipper and pushed the denim over my ass. Then he squeezed my cheeks through my boxer briefs and jutted his hips forward in a manic quest for friction. His heavy breathing and twitchy fingers indicated he was in the same frantic condition as me.

"Lie down, Der."

I turned on the lamp next to my bed, then sat on the edge of the mattress and kicked off my shoes before shucking my jeans aside. My boxer briefs left nothing to the imagination, but the scrap of cotton covering my junk represented a last barrier. A gentle reminder that I could change my mind at any moment. Maybe he'd lie beside me and I'd finally snap out of this trance. Maybe this was a prolonged bi-curious episode and not the sexual awakening I thought it might be.

Fuck, I hoped not.

My mouth went dry the moment he pushed his shirt over his shoulders. He was a god. His smooth olive skin and perfectly toned abs were a thing of beauty. He dropped his shirt on the floor, then gave me a sultry smile as he unbuckled his belt. I licked my lips hungrily. The sight of a bare-chested Gabe with his jeans undone made me feel dizzy. It took everything I had not to reach for my cock and jack myself when he unzipped and then lowered his jeans and stepped out of them.

"Christ, you're beautiful," I whispered without thinking.

Gabe grinned as he climbed onto the bed. He stretched out beside me, rolled to his side, and set his hand on my hip.

"So are you." He put his finger on my lips before I could argue. "Shh. Is this okay?"

I nodded, loving that he'd repeated my question. He was nervous too. "Yes, but...we could do more."

"Like what?"

I let out an amused huff. "Dude, I have no fucking clue. Don't ask me what comes next."

"Such a smartass," he teased, reaching out to trace my eyebrow. "Kiss me."

"Yes," I agreed, sidling closer to him.

Gabe met me halfway and pressed his lips against mine. I sighed into the sweet connection. I loved the hint of scruff on his chin and the heat of his body. He seemed to know exactly how much pressure to apply. Not too hard and never too soft. The only problem was my insatiable craving for more. I waited for him to plunge his tongue into my mouth and take over, but he seemed content to go slowly. Maybe he wanted me to make a move.

I flattened my hand over his right pec, then let it drift to his hip before pulling him against me and nudging my knee between his thighs. Gabe hummed his approval and sprang into action. He cupped the back of my head and drove his tongue inside as he rolled on top of me. We broke the kiss with a gasp of pleasure. He was rock hard, and I was throbbing with need. Our combined arousal was a heady thing. And when he shifted his weight so his cock slid alongside mine, I was ready for more.

Gabe slid his fingers under the elastic of my briefs and eyed me cautiously.

I tilted my head in acquiescence. "Keep going."

He rose above me and sat back on his heels. Then he slowly lowered the fabric over my shaft. He glanced up at me reverently, licking his lips in a show of approval when I lifted my hips and pushed my briefs out of the way. I plucked at his until he got the message.

"Take them off me," he commanded in a husky tone.

I obeyed without question. I splayed my hands over his ass, arched my back, and rubbed my bare cock against his. An electric current went through me. I'd never felt anything like it. Just looking at us...naked and hard for each other, was like a dream. And when his precum dripped onto my shaft, I shivered.

Gabe braced his weight on one hand and gripped his dick and tapped it against mine.

I set my feet on the mattress and bucked my hips upward, wordlessly looking for more of everything. "Oh, fuck. Can I touch you?"

"You don't have to ask, Der. You can do whatever you want," he assured me, bending to capture my mouth in a rough kiss.

The extra spark in the connection gave me the courage to do exactly as he suggested. I reached between us and for the first time in my life, I touched another man's rigid cock. Gabe pulled back slightly and nodded in encouragement.

"You're big," I commented, wrapping my fingers around his

girth. I tested his length and thickness before stroking him languidly. "Does this feel good?"

"Yeah. Really good," he choked. "Let me...let me touch you too."

I might have actually whimpered when he gripped me firmly and squeezed. And when he brushed his thumb over my slit and smeared precum over the mushroom head, then jacked my cock like a pro, I cried out. Gabe kissed me again. Probably to shut me up. I didn't mind at all. This fucking gorgeous man with his tongue in my mouth hovering over me with his hand on my dick, stroking me while I did the same to him...this was heaven. When he increased the pressure just a tad, I felt a familiar tingle at the base of my spine and knew I wouldn't last long.

"Gabe, I'm—I'm close," I said, breaking the kiss.

He bit my bottom lip, then slid down my chest and kneeled between my thighs. He took over stroking both of us, twisting his wrist at each turn. I wanted to comment on his technique, but I couldn't speak coherently. I let him take over. I'd happily go wherever he led at that moment. Though I had to admit I was shocked when he leaned down and swallowed me whole.

I'd been on the receiving end of my share of blowjobs but nothing like this. Gabe knew what he was doing. He pulled back to lick me from base to tip, sucking the head of my cock while he kneaded my balls. Then he glanced up at me briefly and angled his head to take more of me. I pulled his hair and lifted my hips rhythmically. When he moved his hand from the inside of my thigh and brushed his thumb over the sensitive skin above my hole, I couldn't hold on.

My orgasm washed over me in a fierce wave. It was too late to warn Gabe. He pulled back but not quite in time. Cum shot across his bottom lip and his chin, then my stomach. I started to apologize for the lack of notice, but I couldn't catch my breath. Just when I thought I could speak, Gabe kneeled above me, jacking his cock like crazy. He came with a roar a moment later.

He closed his eyes and shook like a leaf, holding my knee for purchase until he regained control. Then he opened his eyes and grinned. My heart somersaulted and burst with joy. I laughed at the exhilarating sense of lightness. I felt like I was soaring through clouds and yet grounded and safe at the same time.

We were cautious with each other afterward, as though we sensed the fragility in this new thing between us. We cleaned up together in the bathroom. I ran the shower and gestured for him to go first. He held a towel for me when I stepped out and motioned for me to turn so he could dry my back. The simple gesture conjured a new round of butterflies. I didn't know why I was nervous to touch him after what we'd done. But I was pathetically grateful he had no such reservations. When we fell back onto my bed naked, it didn't feel weird to curl up next to him.

"Are you thirsty?" I whispered.

"No, I'm all right. Are you?"

"Yeah. I mean...I'm not thirsty. I—this feels strange. We just... you know." I gestured between us manically.

"Had sex," he supplied.

I frowned as I propped my head on my elbow. "But we didn't... you know...*do* it."

"Fuck?" Gabe chuckled. "True. But I sucked your dick, and that's definitely a form of *doing* it."

I lowered my head to hide my blush, then nodded. "That was hot. I—how did we get here?"

He set his thumb under my chin and gave me a searching look. "Are you okay with this? Do you want me to go?"

"No," I replied swiftly. "Stay."

"Just so you know...we're not doing anything wrong. It might be complicated, but it's not wrong."

"Which part is complicated?"

"We're teammates. I've never been with a guy who plays the same sport as me. Ever."

I nodded in agreement, though at that moment being in the

same sport and on the same team was the least of my worries. I was buck-ass naked in bed with a man. A really fucking sexy man.

"Who have you been with? Have you had boyfriends?" I widened my eyes dramatically before continuing, "Do you have one now?"

"No, dummy. I don't have a boyfriend." Gabe smoothed my hair and then tugged it playfully. "You're cute when you get anxious. You ask a lot of questions."

"I'm not anx—fine. I'm anxious."

"If it makes you feel any better, I am too."

"It helps," I admitted. "But you've been here before, right?"

"Yes, but it's been awhile. I had a boyfriend my senior year of high school and another one last year."

"Oh. What about girls?"

"I've been with a few but nothing serious. Most of my real relationships have been with guys. The last one was probably the most serious I'd ever been with anyone. We broke up six months ago and...it sucked."

"What was his name?" I asked for no particular reason.

"Marco."

Great. I hated Marco.

"What happened?"

"He graduated and he wanted to come out. It was kind of our plan, but I...I couldn't do it. I wasn't ready. I'd just made the national team, and I couldn't throw away my chance at a shot to go to the Olympics. The Olympics are a couple of years away still. I thought he'd be cool waiting a little longer, but...he wasn't." Gabe shrugged with faux nonchalance.

"I'm sorry."

"Whatever. It's old news."

"I thought you switched schools to be closer to where the national team practices," I said, frowning.

"That was part of it. Marco was the other part."

"Oh." I bit my lower lip, confused by the sting of jealousy. "Who else knows you're bi?"

"My mom. That's it."

"And she's cool with it?"

Gabe let out a half laugh. "She says she is, but I think she hopes this is my *bi-curioso* phase."

I smiled wanly. "It's not?"

"Doubtful. Lately I've been thinking I'm gay. I'm just not as turned-on by girls. My efforts never work out for me the way they do for my straight friends. Chelsea's party is a great example. I kissed your ex at the beginning of the night but ended up with your jizz all over my underwear."

"Jizz? That's such a gross word," I said primly.

"Do you like cum better?"

"That's kind of gross too."

"All right. How about semen?"

I snickered. "Too clinical."

"Picky, picky. Spunk? Love glue? Cock snot?"

I threw my head back on the pillow and burst into laughter. "Cock snot?"

Gabe waggled his brows, then leaned in and bit my bottom lip. "Well, I gave you choices. Which one?"

"Cum is fine."

He lifted my hand and kissed my knuckles. "Your cum tastes amazing."

"Oh, my God. I'm not ready for cum talk," I groused, closing my eyes.

Gabe chuckled, scooting closer to me so his half-hard cock rested against mine. He squeezed my ass until I looked at him. "I'll be good. I don't want to scare you away now. I've had a crush on you for a while. I figured you were straight and that I never had a chance. To be here with you right now...this is fucking amazing."

"Yeah. It is," I agreed. We stared at each other with matching sappy smiles for a moment until I added, "We're not telling anyone, right? I mean, you're not out and I—"

"Did you want to come out?" he asked, looking slightly alarmed.

"No way! I'm not ready. I need some time to adjust. I'm assuming you want to keep quiet too."

"Yeah. I need to keep my head down and play well. No personal drama."

"Do you really think anyone cares?"

"Some might. My dad would for sure. I want to say I don't care, but I'm not ready to deal with the bullshit."

"That works for me. We can find excuses to be together...I mean, if you want," I added.

"I want," he said in a sultry tone that turned me inside out.

I traced his lip with the tip of my finger and whimpered when he sucked the digit greedily. "Mmm. I—can we do it again?"

He chuckled, then hooked his leg over my thigh and pumped his hips. "Fuck, yeah."

I moaned with pleasure at the renewed friction and sealed my mouth over his as Gabe rolled on top of me. I'd never given up control to a lover, but I instinctively let Gabe lead. I liked the feel of his weight. He was strong yet lithe. He moved over me forcefully, the way he did in the water. But here I could give in and let go.

And something in that surrender felt like my first true taste of freedom.

4

Within a couple of weeks, fall semester and the regular water polo season were in full swing. The schedule was grueling. I began my day at the crack of dawn, jumped into the pool, went to school for a few hours, then got back into the pool or onto a bus bound for a game or a tournament at another university somewhere in So Cal. By the time I finally arrived home, I was freaking exhausted and I usually still had some studying or reading to do before I crashed for the night. I'd been doing a variation of this routine since I was in junior high school. The long days and physical fatigue hardly fazed me. In fact, I kind of got off on the adrenaline rush. But Gabe was a game changer.

His presence added an element of danger I found simultaneously exciting and scary as hell. As he'd pointed out, the biggest challenge was being on the same team and pretending our friendship was a gradual thing. I was a terrible actor. Feigning indifference when Gabe walked into a room wasn't easy.

I'd always thought he was attractive, but his looks were only part of his appeal. Gabe exuded confidence. And let's face it, there was nothing quite as sexy as self-assurance with the right amount of swagger. Some days I was sure I'd give myself away. He didn't have to do much to make my heart beat like a drum. The sight of him walking onto a pool deck in a low-slung Speedo that left little to the imagination was enough to turn me on.

Gabe seemed better at compartmentalizing this new thing between us. When he was in the pool, he was focused and centered. He might be funny and engaging in the locker room but once we hit the water, he gave his all and expected the same from everyone on the team. Including me. That wasn't exactly an issue. I tended to be as serious in the pool as I was in everyday life, which was probably part of why I was chosen to be team captain. I was a hard worker, but Gabe was the natural-born leader.

His love of the game showed in everything he did. He was an asset at the net with a fierce cross-cage shot that always seemed to take the other team by surprise, and he never backed down on defense. He had a habit of pumping his fist in the air and then smacking the water when he made a goal. I'd hated it when we were opponents and I was the guy he'd scored on. Now, it made me laugh. He was equally supportive of everyone else's achievements. He whooped and cheered his fellow teammates for a job well done with an innate joy that was truly inspirational.

Sometimes I couldn't believe he was mine. Well...secretly mine. I'd find myself staring at him from across the locker room, lost in a state of admiration and longing. Occasionally he'd catch my eye, and I swore it took everything I had to stay focused and pretend he was just one of the guys. Not easy when my mind conjured visions of him on his knees while he sucked my cock.

We figured it would seem more natural if we were politely indifferent in front of our teammates in the beginning. After a while, they'd assume we'd put our differences aside and become buddies. By the end of September, we decided we'd passed the "friendship" test and gave ourselves permission to spend as much time together as we wanted.

We were inseparable. We shared meals in between practices.

We took turns walking each other to class, and then we'd text afterward and agree on a location to meet before heading off to a second practice together. Gabe would come over after the final game or practice of the day, I'd make us something to eat or he'd grab something on the way back to my place, and we'd curl up on the sofa and watch television with our feet tangled under the coffee table.

On nights I was sure Evan would be out late, we were braver. We'd lie in each other's arms, pausing the action on the screen to grope and make out until the desire to be naked became too strong to ignore. Then we'd head to my room, lock the door, shed our clothes, and come together in a passionate frenzy. And every time seemed better than the last.

I couldn't believe what I'd been missing. I loved the feel of his stiff cock against mine. I loved touching him, holding him, and within a few short weeks, I'd become obsessed with learning how to give a decent blowjob. My Google search engine was an embarrassing treasure trove of "how-to" tips about pleasing your man. The perfectionist in me demanded that I be as informed as possible. Some of the online articles I read were helpful reminders to relax your jaw, mind your teeth, and one said humming while bobbing your head was a good thing. I shifted in my seat uncomfortably. Jesus, I couldn't even sit in class without thinking about sex. I cast my gaze from the white screen at the front of the lecture hall to the penis doodle in the corner of my open notepad.

Oops. I flipped the page over quickly and gave a sideways glance at the student next to me, who thankfully seemed engrossed in the professor's spiel about the future of global economics. I started to turn when I noticed a familiar face a few seats away. I craned my neck and—what the hell?

Amanda.

I'd seen her at a few parties and around campus, but we hadn't talked since Chelsea's fateful end-of-summer bash back in August. What the hell was she doing in this class? Sure, there were more than three hundred students here, but I couldn't believe I hadn't noticed her. Even if she'd transferred, I should have seen her by now. I wondered why she hadn't said hello. Maybe she'd decided the "ex-to-friends" thing wasn't going to work. Not something I could worry about. I was here to learn, I reminded myself as I reopened my notebook to the penis doodle page. I flipped to a clean page just as my cell vibrated in my pocket.

How's class?

I stared at Gabe's text for a few seconds, then glanced up at the professor briefly before replying.

Boring. Why aren't you in biology?

I am. It's mega boring. Like watching paint dry.

Mine is too except I just noticed Amanda is in this class too. And she's sitting five seats away from me. I didn't notice her until today.

Gabe sent a series of surprised-faced emojis. *Do you think she's following you?*

Doubtful

Just don't flirt with her.

I sent him a smiley face emoji. *Don't worry.*

Gabe responded with a flurry of hieroglyphic emojis that would probably take the rest of class to unravel. Then he followed it up with a single heart and, *See you at practice, Ebab.*

I frowned at the screen. *What's ebab?*

Babe backward. I'm just trying it out. What do you think?

Weird. I like it.

I like you.

My pulse skittered. They weren't *those* three words, but they still seemed significant. I held my finger over my keyboard and wracked my brain for a non-threatening way to say, "I'm so fucking obsessed with you in a not-creepy way." I typed and erased "me too," "same here," and even a lame-ass "cool" before repeating his sentiment.

I like you too. And then I added, *Ebab*

I pushed Send and held my breath. Then I turned off my cell and stuffed it in my backpack.

Geez, what was happening to me? I'd never been this tangled up inside over a girl. I wanted to be near him all the time. He was commanding yet approachable. I'd never met anyone as passionate as him. He truly had a lust for life. Gabe wasn't capable of casual interest. If he liked something or someone, he gave his all. To be the someone he thought of outside of the pool was...electrifying. He sparked something in me I'd never felt before.

Definitely not with Amanda.

I snuck another sideways glance her way. Amanda was pretty and sweet and easy to be around. But I hadn't burned for her. Not like I did for Gabe. We were together for two years...six months too long. Surely she had to think we'd devolved into a boring habit too. Our conversations were centered around water polo and our schedules and the sex was just okay. I remembered thinking I had to end it after the holidays, but I didn't know how to do it without hurting her. In the end, breaking up was as awful as I thought it would be. Eventually, she agreed we could just be friends but so far, we hadn't managed to do that. The fact that I was uneasy sitting a few seats away from her in a crowded lecture hall made me think we might never get there.

I refocused and took copious notes for the remaining hour of class. When it was over, I made my way to the exit and of course, immediately bumped into Amanda. She greeted me with a tight smile that went nowhere near her eyes.

"Hi, Derek. How are you?"

"Uh...I'm good. You? I haven't seen you in a while. It's funny to bump into you here. I didn't know you were in this class," I babbled. *Fuck. Let the nonstop chatter commence.* I willed myself to shut up and give her a chance to talk.

She pushed a wayward strand of golden hair behind her ear

and nodded. "I transferred in two weeks ago. I waved at you a couple of times, but you didn't see me."

"Huh. Sorry. I must have been engrossed in the lecture," I joked.

"Right. How's polo? I caught your game last weekend. Good win."

"Yeah, thanks. It's going well. Uh...I should go. I've got pract—"

"Things seem to be working out with Gabe," she intercepted.

I nodded slowly. "Yeah, better than expected. He's awesome."

"He is. It's nice that you've become such...good friends." Her extra emphasis on those last two words unnerved me.

I inclined my head and stepped backward. "We are. I'll see—"

"I've heard things about him," she continued in a rush.

"What kind of things?" I prodded irritably.

Amanda gave me an insipid smile as she hiked her designer bag higher on her shoulder. I noted the way her blue stone earrings matched her cardigan. There was a time I would have admired her attention to detail. She would have blushed prettily and thanked me but oddly enough, I wasn't so sure it was a compliment anymore. It was simply an observation. I couldn't say why, but the matching colors struck me as a little too perfect.

My nod of appreciation had more to do with my craving for order. Words and concepts like coordinating, complementing, and harmonious were like crack to me. My desire to color inside the lines and not upset the flow was a big part of why I'd been attracted to Amanda. We were all surface. We never really knew each other, and we never would.

And now her vaguely accusatory tone put me on high alert and made me want to get the fuck away from her, ASAP.

"He's a little...free and easy. Open to exploration, if you know what I mean. He likes you. Anyone can tell. Even Chelsea noticed it. Who knows? Maybe he's just real friendly. Either way...be careful, Der." She waved before turning away, leaving me in a haze of designer perfume and innuendo.

I watched her head in the opposite direction then turned on my cell and dialed Chelsea's number. There was a good chance she wouldn't pick up. We never called each other. We'd had numerous conversations about how almost everything could be and should be communicated via text.

"This better be good, Der. I'm mid-pedi and you're ruining my *feng shui* moment," she snarked.

"Did you tell Amanda about me and Gabe?" I blurted.

"Why would I do that? I didn't know there was a 'you and Gabe' and even if I did, I would assume you'd be the one doing the telling. Not your ex-girlfriend. What the fuck's going on?"

I gave Chels a brief rundown of my chat with Amanda as I made my way across campus. I pushed my hand through my hair and let out a beleaguered sigh. "And why is she suddenly in one of my classes? We've never had a class together."

"Sounds like she's up to something, Der, but I swear I've never talked to her about you or Gabe. I didn't know there was anything to talk about. You haven't said a word. Are you guys like boyfriends?" she asked quizzically.

"I don't know...maybe."

I held the phone away when she squealed gleefully. "Oh, my God! Cuteness overload. Spill the tea, Der. I want to hear everything!"

"Spill the what?"

"The tea! The gossip! Ugh. You're going to need some gay coaching. I'll assign Mitch. He's your go-to homo. He can give you any cultural reference and—"

"Whoa. Hold up. I don't want to talk to Mitch, and I don't want to tell you anything else. I'm sorry, Chels but...I need this to be mine for now. And it needs to be on the DL. Don't say a word to anyone. Promise?"

"I promise." She waited a beat, then said, "You really like him."

"I do. And I don't want to mess it up."

"You won't. You're amazing. A real catch. If he's smart, he knows it too." Chelsea sighed dreamily. "Now let me go before I get kicked out with wet toes. No one likes a phone talker at a nail salon. Love you, Der."

She hung up before I had a chance to reply. I paused in front of the aquatic center and shoved my phone into my bag. I nodded absent greetings to a few friends heading toward the pool, but I didn't join them right away. My head was spinning. I trusted Chelsea. She wouldn't say anything about Gabe and me. And she was probably right about Amanda. I doubted my ex knew anything, but the thought of her spying on me was creepy as hell. She was right about one thing, though. I had to be more careful.

TRUE TO HIS WORD, Coach paired Gabe and me together for practice drills and passing exercises. A couple of weeks into our "forced" friendship, he laid off and probably wouldn't have cared if we switched things up on our own. We were grown adults, and he wasn't paid to babysit us. He was paid to win. And with Gabe on board, we were a freaking winning machine. Everyone acknowledged that Gabe's presence in the pool made us all better players. His spatial awareness was uncanny. He knew when to pass and when to hold, and his arm was a damn cannon. Even the best goalies flinched when Gabe cocked his arm back to shoot the ball.

I snickered at Troy's colorful play-by-play about our last win of the weekend. A few of us huddled around a small low table in the hotel lobby bar, adding commentary where necessary. Troy was our set guard. He was a burly guy with curly brown hair and a contagious sense of fun. Gabe and I were supposed to room with Jason and him tonight. Jason had already gone upstairs to crash. I'd been tempted to go with him, but there was a science to rooming with three other guys. The first person always went for the rollaway and left the rest to fight over who got their own bed. Usually we had three per room, but there'd been a snafu at the hotel and rather than try to find another hotel to accommodate us, we opted for cozy and a big discount.

The moment Gabe realized what might happen, he gave me a knowing look and tapped his bag against my hip in a silent communication that translated to "you and me." I wasn't so sure that sharing a bed with two other guys in the room was a great thing. What if we fell asleep with our arms around each other? Gabe was a cuddly person. On the rare occasions he spent the night at my place, I'd wake up with him plastered to my back. It took some getting used to in the beginning. His warmth and size overwhelmed me sometimes. I loved it now. But not with an audience.

"...and then I lobbed it over Taylor's head. Fuckin' amazing, dude," Troy said, stifling a yawn. "How are we working the sleeping sitch?"

"Does it really matter?" Gabe asked before lifting his water glass for the waiter to refill.

"Maybe not. I'm so tired, I don't think I'd notice if a hot chick climbed in my bed tonight. I'm going upstairs now. You coming?" Troy stood and pulled his duffle bag over his shoulder.

"In a minute," Gabe replied.

"Same here. I want to finish my nachos," I said.

Troy made a dubious face at the congealed mess of cheese and sour cream on the plate in front of me, then gave us a peace sign and sauntered toward the bank of elevators near the bar area. When he was out of sight, Gabe nudged my knee and then rolled his eyes.

"You're the world's worst liar, Der."

I chuckled. "I know. God, I wish we could drive home tonight. How are we gonna do this? Maybe if I put a pillow between us—"

"Don't worry. I can keep my hands to myself for one night."

I went quiet for a moment. "Do you think they suspect anything? It's been almost two months. I feel like it's getting harder to act normal and that I'm going to accidentally give us away. I just really don't want it to happen in a San Diego hotel room with two teammates. Maybe I should just sleep with Troy tonight," I huffed.

"No way. You're mine," Gabe growled.

I blinked in surprise, then smirked. "No need for jealousy. He's not my type."

"Good." He covered a yawn and slumped in his chair. "We need to kill fifteen minutes before we head upstairs. Tell me a story or give me a trivia question or something to keep me awake."

I picked up my cell and scrolled to a trivia app. "General, music, sports, Minecraft?"

"I suck at Minecraft. Anything else is cool."

We went back and forth, peppering each other with a range of questions like "What model car followed Ford's Model T?" and "What does a Richter scale measure?"

I stifled a yawn and asked, "Who directed the first Harry Potter movie?"

Gabe squinted as though in deep thought, then replied, "Hufflepuff."

I snickered and shook my head. "Not even a choice. Try again."

"Oh, you're withholding choices. Hmm. I got this, babe. Voldemort." He slapped his hand on the table and grinned.

"Wrong again, and you slipped," I said, giving him a sharp look.

"Huh?"

"You called me 'babe.' "

"I did?"

"Yeah."

"Sorry. I wish Ebab sounded less awkward. I'm not even sure how to pronounce it. Long e or short e?"

I smiled and stood. "Long, I think. C'mon. They're probably asleep now."

Gabe followed me to the elevators. "I need to come up with something else. Whatever it is, it can't be schmoopy."

"Schmoopy?" I repeated with a laugh, stepping into the elevator.

"Yeah. No honey, sweetheart, love dumpling...those are all out."

"That's a good thing," I commented. I waited for the doors to close, then backed him against the wall and licked his lips. "I like 'babe' the best. Save it for when you can say it out loud."

Gabe grabbed my face in his hands and thrust his tongue into my mouth. The kiss was abbreviated but hot as hell. I sucked in a gulp of air and tried to step back. Gabe yanked at my sweatshirt and then traced my jawline lovingly. It took everything I had not to melt in a puddle of goo when he whispered, "Babe."

I shivered and wrapped my arms around myself when the doors slid open. "Maybe we shouldn't sleep together."

"Shh. It'll be okay," he said softly.

It was hell.

I'd never been more aware of another person in my life. We spent so much time acting like buddies that the one place we were free to explore this new thing between us was in bed. When we occasionally spent the night with each other, we made up elaborate stories about needing to get to practice early in case our roommates called us out. But we went out of our way to avoid running into Evan or Brent, so it was never an issue anyway.

Lying in a glorified full-sized bed with two other guys in the room was an unprecedented challenge. There wasn't enough room on the mattress to divide the sleeping space and remove a little temptation. I had to suck it up.

"Are you awake?" he whispered, setting his hand on my hip.

I shook my head and rolled to my back. "Yes. What are you—"

"Shh. Don't wake them up. Just relax." Gabe licked the shell of my ear and stroked my cock through my boxer briefs.

"I can't rela—"

Gabe tightened his grip on my shaft and pushed me onto my side. He slid behind me and molded his chest to my back, then reached around to lower my briefs before stroking my dick. I shivered at the contact and backed up so that his rigid length nudged my ass repeatedly.

"Feels good, doesn't it?"

I couldn't answer. Yeah, it felt amazing. His bare cock riding my crack made me want things I never in a million years would have considered until Gabe came along. And when he stuck his finger in my mouth and then set it over my hole while he moved his hips suggestively, I had a feeling it was just a matter of time before I begged him for more.

"Gabe, I—"

"I know, baby. It's okay. Come," he whispered.

My orgasm slammed into me the second he slipped his finger inside. I squeezed my eyes as white light blinded my vision.

It took a few moments for my pulse to return to normal. I fought the urge to turn around and pull Gabe into my arms. It wasn't easy. I laid my hand on his before tiptoeing to the bathroom to clean up. Of course, he followed me.

Gabe closed the door behind him and locked it, then swooped to hug me from behind. He rested his head on my shoulder and looked at our reflection in the mirror.

"That was hot," he murmured.

"Yeah, but we shouldn't have done it. We have to be more careful," I admonished, kissing his cheek.

"We're very careful. And I'm still really horny. Feel my dick."

"I feel it." I licked the column of his throat and purred.

"I want to fuck you so bad. You better tell me your favorite fruit or something."

"Fruit?" I scrunched my nose and gave him a "What the fuck?" look.

"Mine is watermelon. Play along, babe. I'm trying to control myself." He slipped his bare cock between my ass cheeks and rocked his hips back and forth.

"Cherries." I chuckled.

Gabe groaned in my ear. "Cherries suck. They have pits."

"So do watermelons," I whisper laughed. "What are you doing?"

"I'm pretending I'm in your ass. Bend over the sink. Show me your hole."

I met his reflection in the mirror and gulped. Gabe was in a sensual zone. He licked his palm, then wrapped his fist around his cock and stroked himself while he waited for me to obey. I'd never done anything like this before. I was prepared to suck him or help him jack off, but to just spread myself out for him was somehow a million times more decadent.

So I did it.

My spent cock twitched with renewed interest as I pulled my cheeks apart and set a finger next to my entrance. "Like this?"

"Oh, my God, I want to fuck you," he growled in a low sexy voice. "I can't believe what you do to me."

"I want it too, but I've never done it."

"I can make it good for you, baby."

I narrowed my gaze and studied him thoughtfully. "Do it now. Fuck me," I whispered.

That stopped him. For a second, anyway.

He grabbed my ass cheek and jacked his cock furiously. Then he dropped his forehead to my shoulder and shuddered as his release hit him. I felt his cum on my lower back a moment later. He let go of himself and held me against him tightly, rocking his hips until the trembling stopped.

"Holy fuck," he moaned.

"Why didn't you do it?" I asked, turning to face him.

Gabe grabbed a few tissues from the counter and motioned for me to face the mirror again. He wiped his cum from my back, then used more to clean himself. "This isn't a Nike inspirational ad moment. You can't just *do* it. We need lube and time. Especially since you've never done it before. Trust me, it's a bad idea to rush a good thing."

"But you want to do it, right?"

"Yes. I do."

"Which way? I mean...who does what? Which do you like better?" I asked in a hushed tone.

"If you mean 'top' or 'bottom,' I've done both."

"Oh." I mulled the info over and did my best to push the instant bout of jealousy aside. If I thought of Gabe with anyone else, I might actually go insane. Not good.

"I prefer to top, but I'm open to either. No pressure, Der. We won't do anything you aren't ready for."

"I feel ready. Or I will be soon."

"Good. Me too."

Gabe pulled me into his arms and held me close. In spite of the conversation we'd just had, there was nothing overtly sexual in the way he ran his fingers along my spine. It felt comforting and sweet. Like something a boyfriend would do.

The lines had blurred in the past couple of months. I felt more fluid and secure about my sexuality than ever. It was liberating. I wanted to be with Gabe in every way possible. I wanted him in me, surrounding me. I didn't want order and clean lines. I craved his brand of chaos. He scared me sometimes and he pushed my limits, but I'd never felt more clearheaded and self-aware. And I'd never been more sure of anything or anyone in my life.

5

The following weekend, we finished a three-game tournament early Saturday evening and hung out at a local pizza parlor with our teammates for a while before heading back to my house. Evan texted the address of a party he was going to with some friends from his football team and invited me to join him later. Not happening.

If Gabe and I had the house to ourselves, we weren't going anywhere. We gave each other hand jobs in the shower, then dressed in boxer briefs and lay on the sofa with our legs entwined and watched *Game of Thrones* reruns until we started to drift to off. We headed for my room sometime around midnight, locked the door, and fell asleep. I heard Evan come home an hour or more later. It sounded like he was talking to someone. I hoped so. If Evan got laid, he'd be less concerned about my private life. Not that he'd said anything. We were both too busy with our sports and classes to hang out. I had to make a better effort, I mused as I draped my arm over Gabe's stomach and closed my eyes.

I woke up a few hours later with my lover's mouth on my dick. Fuck, there was something so incredible about slowly being coaxed to life with Gabe's talented tongue. It didn't take much for my orgasm to pull me under. I planted my feet flat on the mattress and held his head when I came. Gabe milked me dry, then rose above me and sealed his lips over mine, thrusting his tongue inside. I loved tasting myself on him and he knew it.

I pushed him onto his back, lowering myself until the tip of his dick hit my chin. I gripped him at the base and studied his girth for a moment before licking him like a lollipop. I was a novice at the art of giving a decent blowjob, but his hum of approval was encouraging.

"Fuck baby, that's good," he groaned loudly.

I glanced up and set my finger over my lips in warning before swallowing as much of him as I could. I stroked and sucked, pausing occasionally to fondle his balls. My skills may have been lacking but I made up for it with enthusiasm, bobbing my head while Gabe ran his fingers through my hair. I figured it was safe to do what I liked. Gabe seemed to agree. He lifted his hips and let out a muffled cry of warning. I sucked harder and didn't stop until he pushed my forehead. Then I crawled over him and laid on his chest.

Gabe rolled over, switching positions and bucking his pelvis playfully. I felt him harden against my stomach. Not enough that he'd want to come again but enough to create a delicious friction. I raised my ass slightly and shivered when his length grazed my hole. I held his face between my hands and gave him a hungry look.

"I want to feel you inside me."

Gabe widened his eyes and licked his lips. "Now?"

I reached down and squeezed his semi-erect cock, chuckling when he flinched. "Can you?"

Gabe shook his head and rolled to his side. "I can barely breathe right now. Give me ten minutes."

I hooked my leg over his and shifted to face him. "Should I time you?"

"Such a smartass. Who knew? Actually, I did. You act calm

and collected outside of the pool, but I always suspected you were a little fiery."

"Fiery? Like hotheaded?" I asked dubiously. I was pragmatic and controlled—not fiery in the slightest, but I liked that he thought so.

"No. Passionate." Gabe traced my eyebrows and cheekbones before leaning in to suck my bottom lip. "You want to know something?"

"Hmm?"

"Every day I want you more. It's never been like this for me," he said softly.

"Me either." I closed my eyes for a second. "I never want this to end."

Gabe frowned. "Why would it end?"

I shrugged. "I don't want anything to change, but I'm going to graduate and you're going to the Olympics. I'm not suggesting we're like your last relationship but—"

"We're nothing like that," he intercepted, furrowing his brow. "And we're not ending. We're beginning, babe."

There was a feverish quality in his eyes that dared me to challenge him. I wasn't a total idiot. I wouldn't bring up the weird looks my ex gave me in class or Evan's questioning stare when I told him I was hanging out with Gabe again. I had a feeling we weren't as inconspicuous as we hoped.

Or maybe I *was* an idiot, I mused when I opened my mouth and asked, "Did he hurt you?"

Gabe's already intense expression went steely. I was instantly reminded of what it felt like to be on opposing teams. His feral gaze was meant to send a warning sign. This topic was off-limits. As it should have been. No one wanted to rehash a painful breakup....But I was beyond curious about the man who came before me.

When the silence stretched on, I figured he wouldn't respond. And then he did.

"We hurt each other. Our expectations didn't match our reality anymore, which I suppose is another way to say we grew apart. We weren't honest about what we wanted. The funny thing about dishonesty is that you think you're protecting something and you end up killing it. You know, I didn't want to tell him I made the national team at first."

"Why not?"

"I don't know. Maybe on some level, I knew we wouldn't make it. Is that what happened with you and Amanda?"

"Yeah," I said softly. "I knew it was over well before I broke up with her. I just didn't know why."

Gabe held my gaze thoughtfully. "Are you okay? You look sad."

I shrugged and kissed his brow. "I'm fine. Want to go to the beach?"

He grabbed my wrist when I scooted to the edge of the mattress. "Hang on. If you're worried about something, you should tell me."

"I'm not worried, but...Gabe, we can't sneak around forever."

"We're fine. We have six weeks left in our season. We got this."

"And then what?"

"Hey." Gabe bent to suck on my left nipple, then sat up. "We'll worry about it when we get there, but nothing has to change. What time is it?"

"Eight forty-five," I replied, running my fingers along his spine. "Evan sleeps until noon on Sundays. Get ready."

Gabe crossed the room to pick up his backpack and frowned. "I need swim trunks. I'm not wearing a banana hammock to the beach."

I pointed at my bottom drawer and told him to choose whatever he wanted. He dug out a pair of multicolored swim trunks and waved them above his head like a flag. Then he stepped into one leg but lost his footing and almost fell on his ass. He regained his balance and shot a comical glance my way before shaking his hips so his flaccid penis swayed from side to side. I chuckled at his antics and pointed at the door.

I wasn't sure I agreed with Gabe, but he had the right attitude. I didn't want to waste a moment worrying about the past or the future and take a chance I might miss out on today.

SOME DAYS AUTUMN in Southern California felt like summertime. According to the calendar it was early November, but the seventy-degree temperature, blue skies, and zero breeze screamed beach weather. We rode bicycles from my house to the boardwalk. Evan and I kept a couple of extra bikes in the garage for friends to borrow to go barhopping or to cruise to the beach. I gave Gabe an old, black three-speed with a basket and snickered at his enthusiastic fist bump when he realized his backpack would fit with the towels and Smashball paddles. We stopped at a small market along the way and bought sandwiches and pre-cut watermelon to snack on before continuing to the beach. Then we locked up the bikes, tossed our belongings on the sand, and ran to the water.

When the first big wave rolled in, we caught it and let the current pull us into the Pacific. Gabe came up for air with a whoop. I laughed when he smacked the water's surface the way he did after he'd made a great play. I swam to his side and impulsively hugged him. There was no one near us, and we were far enough from the shoreline that no one would notice anyway. Nonetheless, I was surprised when he yanked me against him and fused his lips to mine. He pulled back with a grin and pointed to the wave cresting behind him.

"Let's ride this one in. Last one to shore has to massage my feet. Ready? Go!"

He was long gone before I could reply. I had no hope of catching up to him, but I gave it my best effort. Gabe greeted me with a devilish grin before hurrying toward our backpacks. He grabbed the Smashball paddles and a tiny red ball and motioned for me to join him on the wet sand before handing me a paddle.

"I should warn you that I'm really good at this," I boasted. "Evan and I got up to two hundred this summer."

"If that's the world record, we need to beat it."

"That took forever. There's no way you and I can do it in one go."

He adjusted his sunglasses and scoffed. "Not with that attitude."

"I didn't know you were so competitive outside of the pool," I griped.

"I was born this way. Can't turn it off. I'm a firm believer that you should never stop till you get what you're after. And today we're all about chasing number two hundred and one. Let's do this, baby."

Gabe wasn't kidding. He was wildly competitive. We didn't hit our goal the first two tries, but we were getting better. One hundred and seven and then one fifty-three. I made him take a break to eat but agreed to continue the quest afterward.

We spread our towels on the sand and unwrapped our small feast. Gabe tore into his sandwich with gusto. I chuckled at his blissed-out expression and focused on the glitter of sunlight across his handsome face. Damn, he was beautiful. He reminded me of a warrior with his proud carriage and furrowed brow. He was the kind of guy who was willing to work hard and make sacrifices where necessary, but he wouldn't give up. If he set his sights on a goal, he went for it full-board.

"You're really going to the Olympics, aren't you?"

Gabe gave me a shrewd once-over with a roguish grin. "Where'd that come from?"

"I dunno. You don't let go when you get an idea in your head."

He finished chewing, then nodded. "Probably true."

"That means I could be here until midnight playing Smash-ball with you," I groused playfully.

Gabe chuckled. "We're gonna do it, Der. Never a doubt. See, it's all in the way you look at it. You say 'until midnight,' but the real goal is 'until we hit two hundred and one.' Subtle but it makes a difference. One is based on time and the other on achievement. The achievement is the important part. If you can get timeliness to mesh with achievement, even better. So to answer your question...yes. I'm going to the Olympics. I don't know when or in what capacity, but it'll happen."

"I like that you're so sure."

"It's necessary. If you give yourself any wiggle room, some of that desire seeps through and you begin to second guess your purpose, ya know?" he asked, turning to face me.

"Maybe. I've never had a dream that big. Graduating college and finding a job is as big as it gets for me right now. I just don't want to work for my dad."

"What does he do?"

"His firm sells technology services to utility companies. Don't ask me what that means. All I know is, there's no equipment involved and it's supposedly the next big wave in the tech market." I glided my hand over my head to indicate I had no idea what the hell any of that meant.

"Okay, so what do you want to do? Where do you see yourself a year from now? Do you want to stay in the area or move to LA or San Francisco? I know you, Der. You're a planner. You must have ideas."

I nodded. "Yeah, I do. I want to go to culinary school and eventually open my own bistro. My parents won't approve but..."

"But it's your life."

"True, but you've met my folks at our games. You can probably tell what I'm up against," I huffed.

"Yeah. They're a little intense," he conceded.

"That's one way to put it. I either have to prepare to do battle or take the easy way out and just do what they expect. I'm twenty-three, but my desire to please and not rock the boat hasn't gone anywhere. I mean...look at you. The Olympics is a lofty goal, but it's a solid one. A bright shiny coin...or gold medal," I commented with a smile. "Mine is fuzzier. The uncertainty makes me feel like I'm treading water in the deep end of the pool in the dark. I can do it, but I wish I could see."

Gabe tilted his chin thoughtfully. "You use your senses. That's even better. You say you're confused sometimes, but you know when to pay attention. You identify the obstacles and take notes. I like that about you."

"I think that's a nice way of saying I'm overly cautious," I huffed before biting into my sandwich.

"Take a compliment, Vaughn. I think you're cool. I like you and I admire you."

I lowered my sunglasses and flashed a megawatt grin at him. "Thank you. I think you're pretty cool too."

"Aww. Quit it. You're making me blush," he snorted, bumping my arm.

We stared at the horizon, lost in our own thoughts for a moment. I didn't want to talk about uncertain futures anymore, but I was curious about something.

"I thought the Olympics was something your dad wanted. When did it become your dream?" I asked as I reached into my bag for a water bottle.

Gabe furrowed his brow and scratched the back of his neck. "When he had his next kid. I guess I wanted him to remember I was still around."

"Oh."

"He didn't call or come by consistently anymore and...I didn't do well with the rejection. I was angry all the time. One day it came out in my game. I scored five goals, caused five kickouts for the other team and morphed into a freaking Tasmanian devil in the water. I remember my coach pulling me aside afterward and saying, 'Passion is your muse. Use it.' I was maybe eleven. I didn't know what he meant at the time, but I wrote it down. My mom was always doing that to help her learn English and...long story short, my coach was right. The second I rechanneled my anger, I was free. Pretty soon, the sport that dragged me down and highlighted all of my flaws, like my inability to focus, my lack of drive and determination...became my greatest strength. I made the game *mine*. It's not his. It belongs to me. We may share some DNA, but I'm nothing like him. I'm not a quitter."

"Did he quit water polo?"

"No. He quit on his family. He quit on me. He makes guest appearances now like that's a big fucking deal and..."

"And what?"

"It's not. Fuck him," he said in a small voice. "If I ever have kids, I won't be an occasional dad. Maybe water polo isn't everything, but it's helped me become a better person. John Wooden said sports don't build character, they reveal it. I totally believe that's true. Discipline, friendship, hard work. I don't know where I'll be in five years or ten or twenty. Maybe I'll coach, teach or hey...maybe I'll work at my boyfriend's bistro selling—" Gabe tossed a quizzical sideways glance at me. "What are we selling?"

"Baguettes and stuff," I replied, pursing my lips together to keep my smile from expanding too far too fast.

"Cool. I like bread. The point is...I'm going to keep working my ass off, and I'm gonna do my best to be a decent human. That's all."

I swallowed around the lump in my throat, overcome with pride and admiration for him. I felt his pain and his strength as though he'd handed them to me for safekeeping for a moment. He'd left himself open and raw and in that instant, I felt closer to him than anyone else on the planet.

"You're going to be the best, Gabe."

He reached out to lower my sunglasses and then his own. "So are you. Kiss me."

"Here?"

"Yeah. Right here, right now."

I leaned in and brought my lips close to his. It was a featherlight connection, like we were both holding our breaths and waiting for a sign to commemorate something new and significant between us. Then Gabe closed his eyes and gently molded his lips to mine. Neither of us moved for a long moment. We just breathed and listened and let ourselves become that something new.

But when I licked the corner of his mouth, everything changed in a flash. Gabe cradled my face and pushed his tongue inside in a passionate, demanding kiss that left me feeling blissed out and slightly intoxicated. I let out an awkward laugh and rested my forehead against his.

"That wasn't a quick kiss. Anyone can see us," I hummed, not bothering to move away.

"I should probably care, but I don't. Come home with me, or I'll come home with you. I just...I want you, Der."

I backed up, then and studied him for a moment before nodding. "Yes. Let's go."

EVAN PULLED up in front of the house just as we hopped off our bikes and deposited them in the garage. Gabe plucked his backpack from the basket and hooked his thumb toward the street.

"My place."

"Yeah. I'll just drop my stuff off. I should probably shower," I said awkwardly.

"Use my shower."

"Is it bigger?"

"No, but..." Gabe narrowed his eyes and set his hands on his hips. "Wait up. Are you going to dump me 'cause my water pressure sucks?"

I snickered at his flabbergasted expression, loving that he knew how to set me at ease with a sweet smile and a silly joke.

"No. Mine sucks too. I'm just...nervous. We're doing this, aren't we?"

"Yeah, we are. But don't be nervous." He started to put his arm around me but dropped it and shoved his backpack in front of his crotch when Evan walked up the driveway. "C'mon. I'm sportin' major wood right now. Quick good-byes, please."

Evan greeted us with bro fist bumps and a ready grin. "How was the beach?"

"Good. Where've you been?" I asked.

It might have been my imagination, but he looked almost bashful when he replied. "I'm working on a school project. Double secret."

"Oh? Tell us all about it."

"What part of double secret didn't you get? I'll lose my spy card if I divulge confidential info," Evan said with a laugh. "Are you around for dinner? I miss your lasagna, Der. And that banana bread you used to make for Amanda all the time. He put butterscotch chips in it. So good. I'm going through withdrawals. Has he cooked for you yet? He's fuckin' amazing."

"Yeah, he's a great cook. I've had his spaghetti and meatballs and veggie orzo but not lasagna." Gabe replied. "You make a mean grilled cheese too, ba—Der."

"Thanks."

Evan quirked his brow curiously. I held my breath and waited for him to ask when I'd started breaking out my best recipes for a guy I couldn't stand a few months ago and if he'd actually almost called me "babe." Thankfully, Evan let it go. He headed up the path to the front door instead and motioned for us to hurry up.

"Come on. Let's watch the game. We can order pizza or something."

"Um...we can't. We have an early practice. I'm gonna crash at Gabe's and get a ride with him in the morning. My car's been acting weird," I lied.

He regarded me with that same curious look, then shrugged. "Oh. Okay. I'll see ya then."

I waited until Evan disappeared inside the house before I spoke. "I hate lying. It sucks."

Gabe didn't say anything. Confirmation wasn't necessary. Secrecy wasn't thrilling anymore. It was exhausting. And it felt dishonest. Evan deserved better from me.

GABE'S APARTMENT was a Spanish-style relic from the 1970s with low ceilings and vintage features that were so dated, they actually looked chic. Like the macramé wall art above the gray sectional and the bright orange spherical pendant hanging over a white plastic dining table. I didn't get the impression the retro modern vibe was intentional, but it was cool. Best of all, he kept it relatively clean and tidy, I mused, casting my gaze around the open floor plan before setting my backpack on a dining chair.

"Want something to drink?" he asked as he headed for the galley-style kitchen adjacent to the living area. "I'm gonna order pizza. They usually deliver in ten or fifteen minutes. And yeah, I know, a salad for you. Boring vinaigrette on the side, hold the olives."

I stuffed my hands into the pockets of my black sweatshirt I'd thrown on. "Thank you. Maybe we should have stayed for pizza with Evan. I feel like he knows something is up."

"I know what you mean. It's getting harder to behave myself around you in front of an audience. Troy gave me a weird look in the locker room the other day when I put my hand on your shoulder. I have to stop touching you so much. Water okay?"

"Yes, please."

Gabe filled two glasses and handed me one. "I think Brent has beer too, if you want one."

"You'd steal your roommate's beer for me?" I asked with a chuckle.

"Anything for you, baby."

The sultry look in his eyes went straight to my dick. I was suddenly parched. I licked my lips and then gulped half of my water. Then I set my glass down and leaned against the counter.

"Is Brent coming home tonight?"

"He said he was at his parents' for a family dinner. They live in Lake Arrowhead, so we have a few hours." He sidled closer to me and ran his fingers down my neck.

"You look like you want to take a bite out of me," I joked. "I thought we were having pizza."

"Fuck pizza." Gabe stepped between my legs and lined his cock up with mine.

My workout pants and his borrowed swim trunks didn't provide much of a barrier. I groaned when he jutted his hips suggestively. I tipped my head back, allowing him room to lick a trail over my Adam's apple and along my chin before covering my mouth in a searing kiss. When the need for oxygen became a reality, I pulled back and laid my head on his shoulder for a moment. I wondered why the gesture didn't feel odd or emasculating. I'd never leaned on ex-girlfriends the way I did with Gabe. I knew I'd been guilty of stereotyping and assuming a role I thought I was supposed to play in past relationships. It felt incredible to let go and just be myself with him. My newfound sense of freedom was exhilarating. And every day that I became a little more comfortable in my skin, I felt equally stifled by the secrecy. But I wasn't going to worry about that tonight.

I pushed at his chest slightly and then reached out to touch his swollen lips. "Gabe, we should—"

"Shower," he intercepted. "This way."

He held my hand and led me down a short hallway to the bathroom. There wasn't enough room for two grown men to comfortably share the space for long. Gabe turned on the water, then pulled his T-shirt over his head and undid the drawstring on his swim trunks.

I closed the bathroom door and admired the view for a moment. Gabe's body was a thing of beauty. I let my gaze travel down his torso to his V-line. I loved the whole package, but my eyes always lingered on that sexy dip leading south. He caught my stare and smirked. "You coming in?"

He stepped into the bathtub and pulled the navy shower curtain halfway across the bar. I finished undressing and set my clothes on the six inches of counter space available before joining him.

"Let me wash your back." I wrapped my arms around him and wiggled my fingers expectantly.

Gabe handed me a bar of soap, then reached for the shampoo and lathered his hair. "Go fast. The hot water doesn't last long."

I washed his back and reached around to soap up his cock, pausing to nibble on his shoulder. "I love your skin. It's so smooth and...sexy."

Gabe turned abruptly and kissed me hard. He swayed his hips from side to side, so his thick penis tapped my leg. "We have to hurry, baby. Change places with me. I'll take care of you."

I wanted to analyze the sentiment of "taking care," but he didn't give me a chance. He scooted around me until I stood under the warm spray. I laughed at his rough ministrations. Gabe wasn't kidding about hurrying along the action. He kissed me repeatedly as he rubbed shampoo into my hair; then he bit my lip and told me to turn around. He opened the shower curtain and grabbed a tube from the jumble of products on the overcrowded countertop.

"What is that?"

"Lube."

"Are we doing this in here? I don't think I—"

"No, baby. Relax. We've done this part lots of times."

"Not in the shower. Is that waterproof? Is there such a thing? Fuck, I should have researched lube brands. Some must be better than others. I'm gonna Google it and—"

"Der, do you trust me?"

I gulped but nodded immediately. "Yes."

"Good. Turn around. Go on." He smacked my right cheek when I hesitated, and my dick twitched in response.

Fuck, who was I? I'd never gotten off on power plays, and spanking wasn't my kink. Or was it? I turned back to glance at the handprint on my ass and scowled at my lover as he squeezed lube onto his hand. "That hurt."

"And you liked it," he quipped with a roguish grin. "Spread your cheeks, baby. That's it. How does that feel?"

Oh, my God. Amazing. I dropped my head and braced my left hand on the white tile and gripped myself as Gabe slipped the tip of a finger into my hole. The cool gel and warm water and the feel of his skin against me was a heady combination. He tapped his erection against my ass and sucked the water from my shoulder as he pushed his digit farther inside me. I groaned and backed up, wordlessly asking for more. He complied, hooking his finger expertly before adding another.

"Fuck," I whimpered.

"Does that feel good?"

The water cloaked us in a sensual cocoon and highlighted sound and touch. It didn't just feel good, it felt incredible. "Yes. More."

He worked a second finger inside and pushed the tip of a third against my entrance just as the water went cold. Gabe pulled out gently and washed his hands again before turning off the spray. He stepped out of the shower and grabbed two towels. We dried off quickly. I tied the navy towel around my waist as Gabe opened the door and tossed his on the floor.

"This way," he said.

I followed him into the adjacent bedroom. He closed the door behind him, then turned on a bedside lamp. A queen-sized bed with a black-and-white striped duvet and a narrow side table were the only furniture. The white walls were decorated with water polo posters and a giant corkboard lined with evenly spaced personal photos of family and friends. I moved to examine a new one of a selfie we'd taken at a recent tournament just as Gabe pulled me against him and thrust his tongue into my mouth hungrily.

I hummed into the connection and raked my fingernails down his back. We stood naked next to the bed, making out with roving hands and soft sighs. I caught our reflection in the mirror next to his closet. My already aching cock pulsed with need at the sight of us naked together. Gabe followed my gaze and grinned wickedly before squeezing my ass. Our tongues dueled frantically, letting the sweet grind build to a feverish pitch until we were writhing and desperate for friction. He massaged my hole repeatedly as he slid his erection alongside mine and sucked my tongue. Fuck, he felt amazing, but it wasn't enough.

Gabe stepped aside and pushed the duvet to the end of the mattress. He flopped onto the bed, then held his left hand out in invitation while he stroked himself with his right. "C'mere. Let me touch you."

"My turn first."

I crawled between his thighs and pressed kisses down his smooth chest, stopping to lick one nipple and then the other. Gabe hummed his approval as he ran his fingers through my hair. He lifted his hips in a wordless request for me to keep going. I kissed my way south until his prick nudged my chin. I grabbed him at the base and looked up at him before flattening my tongue and licking his shaft up one side and down the other. I briefly sucked on the wide mushroom head, then swallowed as much of him as I could.

Sucking Gabe's cock had become one of my favorite pastimes. I loved the way he tasted and smelled. But more than anything, I loved his responsiveness. He had a way of making me feel like I was a blowjob genius in training. He tilted his hips as he praised my mad skills.

"So good, baby. Fuck, yeah."

I loved that he called me "baby." It was endearing and decadent, something sweet I probably shouldn't allow. But in the heat of the moment, it was just one more thing that turned me inside out. I backed off to catch my breath but continued stroking him in a firm grip with my right hand while I jacked myself with my left. Just as I was about to open my mouth again, he pushed at my forehead. Then he pulled me against him and rolled on top of me. It was almost a signature move. We laughed at how easily he could switch positions sometimes. But tonight...it made me nervous.

"Gabe, wait."

"What is it?" he asked, backing up slightly.

I propped myself on my elbows and gulped. "I did some research about...you know. Um, I think it's supposed to hurt. Does it hurt? I mean...you've been on the receiving end, right? Did you like it?" I hated that I sounded like such a weenie, but my accelerated pulse was making it difficult to breathe.

Gabe braced himself above me and studied me for a moment before falling to his side. He threw his leg over mine and pulled me to face him. "Maybe we should talk first."

I closed my eyes and let out a theatric groan. "I'm sorry. I don't want to fuck this up, but—"

"You're not fucking up anything. You know how it works, right?"

"Yeah, your dick goes in my ass. Seems simple enough, except your dick is fucking huge," I huffed sarcastically.

"Why, thank you very much," he replied in a goofy Elvis impression. When I rolled my eyes, he pinched my ass playfully and nipped my chin. "Everyone's first time is different. We'll go slow. If you want to stop, we'll stop."

I bit my bottom lip and nodded. "Okay. So now what?"

Gabe cupped the back of my neck and sealed his mouth over mine as he pushed me onto my back again. The passionate kiss went a long way toward rekindling the fire my nerves had doused. I hooked my legs over his ass to keep him close and sighed at the delicious feel of his thick cock gliding alongside mine. My stomach was slick with our combined precum, creating a natural lube as we humped against each other like horny teenagers. I tilted my hips just as Gabe lowered himself on his belly and crouched between my legs. He gripped my dick and waited for me to look at him. Then he motioned for me to give him the lube and condom on his nightstand.

I obeyed before lying back on the pillow to watch him.

"You okay so far?"

I licked my lips hungrily. "Yes."

Gabe grinned and swooped quickly to swallow me whole. I gasped at the sensual onslaught as he sucked me like a madman. I heard the click of a bottle cap, but I couldn't focus. He licked my balls while he stroked my cock. And then he gently rubbed a single digit over my entrance, applying just enough pressure to make me want more.

"I'm ready. Put your finger in me."

Gabe kissed the inside of my thigh as he pushed two fingers in my hole. A lightning bolt of pleasure swept through me. He pushed in and out a couple of times, hitting my sweet spot at each pass. I writhed under him, wantonly lifting my hips to meet the friction.

"Okay?"

"Oh fuck, yes. More, please," I groaned.

He eagerly complied, upping the tempo as he simultaneously stroked my dick and finger fucked me. I mumbled his name incoherently, arching my back to meet his thrusts. I was on fire.

And then he pulled away.

I sat up to protest but shut my mouth when Gabe ripped open the condom and rolled the latex over his rigid cock. He locked his gaze on mine as he added lube and pumped himself a few times. Then he scooted close and glided his hard-on along my entrance.

"Look at me, baby." He waited for me to obey before continuing. "Watch me, okay? Remember, you're in control. If you want to stop, I'll stop."

I nodded, then licked my lips nervously. "I'm ready. Do it."

He set his sheathed cock over my hole and pushed. Fuck, that was amazing. "Still good?"

"So good. Are you inside me?"

Gabe let out a strangled-sounding half laugh. "Just the tip."

I chuckled at his exaggerated pained expression. "Gimme more. I want you."

He moved inch by inch, pausing frequently to make sure I was all right. And I was. Sure, it hurt every once in a while, but then a surge of intense pleasure would chase away the pain and send me so close to the brink, I was afraid I'd come before he really started to move. I studied Gabe's features, noting his furrowed brow and the sweat beading on his forehead as he struggled to stay in control. My heart did a funny flip in my chest. I brushed his damp hair from his forehead and kissed it just as his balls hit my ass.

"How do you feel?"

"Good, but maybe you should move and—*oh, fuck. Yes,*" I cried.

Gabe pulled almost all the way out before easing his way back inside. Then he did it again...and again. He took his time, slowly rocking his hips back and forth, setting a slow but steady rhythm.

"Fuck, you feel amazing," he hummed.

And so did he. Or something better than amazing. I didn't have words for how I felt. I was overwhelmed. This was beautiful and raw and more intense than anything I'd ever experienced with a lover. Every push and pull seemed to right the balance. We fit each other so well. The ways we were the same and the ways we contrasted were in perfect harmony, from our similar height and build to the difference in our skin color. And the soulful, sweet way he looked at me as he moved inside me was sheer perfection.

Gabe flattened his chest against mine and captured my lips as he quickened his strokes. My dick was trapped between us now, and the friction we generated felt incredible. The mattress creaked when he picked up speed. We shared a smile at the incessant clink of metal but when he changed his angle, pumping and thrusting his hips wildly, my vision blurred. I knew I wouldn't last.

"I'm close," I whispered as that first tingle of awareness flitted along my spine.

"You go first, baby. Come for me."

Gabe braced himself on one hand and closed his fist around my throbbing cock. And I exploded. Cum shot up my chest and over his fingers. I trembled as I clung to him, burying my face in his neck while I rode out one of the most intense orgasms of my life. Gabe's own release pulled him under a moment later. He collapsed on top of me, bucking his hips and gasping for air. I held him close until he caught his breath and nuzzled my cheek.

Gabe smiled and carefully disengaged from my body. He rolled the spent condom from his cock with a sheepish look. "I better get rid of this. Be right back. Don't go anywhere."

I watched him leave the room and listened as he moved down the hall and into the adjacent bathroom. Then I sat up and looked down at the mess of sweat and cum on my chest in wonder.

We'd actually done it. He'd been inside me. I'd gone years without thinking twice about anal sex to thinking about it all the damn time and wondering how it felt to be connected to someone that way. Now I knew.

I gingerly set a finger over my entrance and—

"I brought you a towel and—fuck, that's hot. I could watch you finger your hole all damn night," Gabe purred in a sex-hazed voice. He swiped the mess off my stomach and then jumped onto the bed beside me.

The blush was instantaneous. "I wasn't fingering myself."

"Oh, sorry. Is there another term for sticking your finger in—"

I pounced on him, straddling his stomach and pulling his hands above his head. The smartass remark I had on the tip of my tongue was reduced to a whimper when he lifted his hips suggestively.

"I loved it," I blurted.

Gabe gave me a lopsided smile as he pulled out of my grasp. Then he gathered me close before rolling sideways so we faced each other. "Me too."

"I probably need a little recovery time, but I want to do it again." I traced his toned abs before meeting his gaze. "And I want to fuck you too. Will you let me?"

"Yes."

"Really? Just like that?"

"Of course."

I pursed my lips and looked away for a moment to gather my thoughts and somehow communicate what I was feeling.

"I...you're special," I blurted lamely.

His tentative smile morphed into a boyish grin. "Yeah?"

"Yeah," I readily agreed before shaking my head. "No, you're more than special. You're extraordinary, and I just—"

I caught myself before I blurted the "I love you" on the tip of my tongue. He'd either think it was a heat of the moment confession, or he'd freak out altogether and the last thing I wanted was to scare him away. I bit my lip and tried to think of a non-threatening way to tell him I'd do anything to be with him.

Gabe threaded his fingers through my hair and kissed my forehead. "You just what?" he prodded.

I gulped and leaned into his touch. "You're my favorite person. I want good things to happen to you."

He gave me a thoughtful stare, then caressed my cheek lovingly. "You're mine too, Der. Want to know a secret?"

I smiled at his signature question. It had a funny way of adding intimacy to our situation since we were, by definition, a secret. "Hmm?"

"If I could have anything in the world, this is all I'd want. Me and you. The rest doesn't matter."

"The Olympics doesn't matter?" I joked. I couldn't help it. His intensity surprised me. I felt a stupid desire to lighten the mood before I pledged my undying love.

Gabe frowned. "The Olympics have nothing to do with us. Water polo has nothing to do with us. We're our own thing, and what we have is special."

I nodded profusely, then smothered him with kisses until he chuckled. When I tickled his sides, he flipped me on my back and pulled my arms over my head. He grinned down at me, panting as he stared into my eyes. I could have sworn I saw everything I felt for him in that look.

Maybe even love.

6

Everything changed after that night. We were closer than ever...like real boyfriends without the fanfare. We didn't change our relationship status on social media. We didn't tell our friends and we sure as hell weren't ready to tell our families, but our already intense chemistry was suddenly off the charts. We were a dominant duo in the pool. I was as aware of his presence in the water as I was on dry land. I knew where to pass the ball to ensure he scored and vice versa. Our teammates and coaches didn't question our close connection in or out of the pool. Superstition alone kept the curious at bay. No one messed with success.

Best of all, we'd become masters at finagling sleepovers without alerting either of our roommates. Brent's parents were in the midst of remodeling their mountain home, so he spent most of his free time helping them. And Evan was busy with football and some secret project he was working on at school. If I wasn't preoccupied with my own secrets, I might have asked a few pointed questions. But I had my own life to worry about.

Although at the moment, it was pretty fucking amazing. I was head over heels in love and lust and admiration for Gabe. And yes, I did say "love." Not to him, of course, but there was no reason to lie to myself. I loved him.

I loved his beautiful mind, his silly sense of fun, his quick wit and boundless energy. I could have listened to him talk for hours about his mom's cooking, his anthropology class, or some dickwad ball hog on the national team. And I could have happily sat on the sideline and watched him glide across the pool, cutting through the water with brisk, even strokes. He mesmerized me. But nothing compared to being naked with him moving inside me. Or me inside him. We did it all and we did it as often as possible, but we still couldn't seem to get enough.

It was harder than it should have been to keep my hands to myself. Gabe was worse than me. He had a habit of linking his pinky finger with mine when he thought no one was looking...in line at the grocery store, walking on the boardwalk, on the team bus. He was famous for stealing kisses in front of random places —like the ice cream store at the mall or the alcove next to a restaurant bathroom. And if I knew him, he'd stick his tongue down my throat the second he parked his car on campus in the packed lot under a tree.

He turned off the engine and took a cursory glance at our surroundings before capturing my face in his hands and kissing me senseless. I swore I saw stars when he finally pulled away.

I fiddled with the zipper on my jacket, clandestinely adjusting my dick as I shot a faux-admonishing look at him. "Someone's going to see us, Gabe."

He rolled his eyes. "Unless they have a high-powered micro-scope and can see through those trees, I doubt it. Everyone's in class and you better get going, or you won't get your favorite seat...unless Amanda saves it for you," he added with a teasing grin.

"Ha. I think she dropped the class. She ignored me at Chelsea's party last weekend, which hopefully is a sign she's moved on. Chels thinks she's seeing someone. Then again, Chelsea thinks everyone is in the midst of a big love affair."

"Does she think we are?" he asked with a lopsided grin.

"She knows we are." I shrugged when he gave me a sharp look. "She's one of my best friends. She won't say a word."

"I've got too many other things on my mind. My biology test this afternoon, my dad's visit this weekend. Did I tell you he's coming for the UCLA game?"

"You mentioned it." More than once.

Gabe claimed his father's attention was a distraction at this point in life, but I had a feeling that wasn't necessarily the case. I knew from experience; it was hard to let go of parental expectation. We were nearing the holidays, and I hadn't told my folks about Gabe and me. They knew we were friends, but I left it at that for the same reason I hadn't told Evan. I was protective of us. I wasn't ready for the real world to give their opinion—good, bad, or indifferent.

"Hmm. Kiss me," he growled, pulling me against him greedily.

I melted into the connection, loving the feel of his scruff on my cheek and his soft lips. I lingered longer than I should have before pushing him back.

"I should go," I said.

"Okay. See you at practice."

I nodded, then took another peek out the windows before leaning in to kiss him once more. It was a brief touch of lips. No big deal. But the urge to add a quick "I love you" was stronger than ever. It made me want to stay there, just to be near him. We didn't have to talk. We could just...be.

I finally opened the car door and stepped outside with an absent wave. It was cooler today than it had been all season. I glanced at the three giant palm trees and two amber trees standing sentry near the econ building. The orange leaves of the amber juxtaposed to the green palms might have been jarring anywhere else in the country, but they were commonplace in Southern California. My thoughts bounced precariously as I made my way along the wide path.

Orange leaves, turkey dinner, holiday shopping...I turned the corner and promptly bumped into someone.

"Oh shoot. I'm sorry. Let me get that. I—" I picked up the book the stranger dropped, then straightened...and froze. "Amanda. Hey. Are you heading into class?"

"Hi. No. Well, yes, I *am* going to class, but mine starts in thirty minutes." She tossed her long hair over her shoulder and glanced back toward the parking lot before flashing a tepid smile.

Something in the tilt of her chin and her stiff posture made me wary. I hooked my thumb toward the lecture hall, wishing I was safely ensconced inside. "I thought you were taking global econ," I said, stepping aside for a student rushing for the door.

"No. I sat in on a few lectures, but...I decided it might not be for me."

I sensed an underlying message, but I sucked at guessing games. "Oh. No wonder I haven't seen you lately."

"I've been around. You just haven't noticed," she replied cryptically. "Water polo games, on campus, at parties..."

"Right. I saw you at Chelsea's last weekend," I said awkwardly as I stepped backward. "Um...I should—"

"Are you gay?" she blurted.

I stopped in my tracks. Blood drained from my face so fast that I felt faint. I swallowed around the cotton balls lodged in my throat and squinted.

"Why are you asking me that?" I hated my wobbly tone but on the other hand, I was surprised I could speak at all.

"I've noticed...things."

I huffed in a lame attempt to suggest she had a great imagination, though my panicky expression probably gave me away. I needed to muster a little bravado. Something that clearly said "think what you want" before I walked away with my head high. Unfortunately my mouth and brain were not in sync.

"What kind of things?"

"You and Gabe are always together. You smile at him all the time, and you touch him a lot."

"Touch him?" I repeated weakly.

"Yes. Arms, shoulders...ass." She sighed theatrically, then pursed her red lips before continuing. "To be perfectly blunt, my question is more of a formality, Derek. I know you're gay...or bi. I just need to hear you say it."

"Why?"

"Because you owe it to me," she snapped.

"Owe you? How do I—"

"I loved you, and you broke my heart. You were so casually cruel with your 'It's not you, it's me' bullshit. I gave you space all summer. I didn't crowd you. I waited for you, but you'd moved on...*with a guy.*" She drew out those three words menacingly, stabbing a painted fingernail at my chest. "I couldn't believe it at first, but I followed you and—"

"You followed me?"

"Yes. I've seen you and Gabe all over town...at the beach, the market, the mall, at parties, and at games."

"We're friends, Amanda."

"Friends who fuck," she countered. "You must be. I've seen you kiss when you don't think anyone is around. Don't bother lying. I just saw you making out in his car a few minutes ago."

"So you've been spying on me," I said in true Captain Obvious fashion.

In my defense, I didn't know what to do or say. My heart was beating against my chest like a fucking jackhammer. Any second now I'd start babbling, if I wasn't careful. I didn't care what she thought about me, but I had to protect Gabe. He was infinitely better at pressure situations than I was, but he wasn't ready to come out. Not now. Not like this.

"I didn't spy, but I've been curious. Trust me, I'm not the only one who's noticed. Your teammates might not say anything to your face, but they suspect something is up. Ask Troy. Or don't. Look, I didn't want to do this here but when I saw you kissing in the parking lot..." Amanda bit the inside of her cheek and sniffed before continuing with a pained expression. "I just want to know if he's the real reason we didn't make it."

I gulped around the rising bile in my throat and gave her a harsh once-over. "Gabe has nothing to do with us. He's my friend and teammate but that's all. Leave him out of this," I growled angrily.

"Hey, I didn't say I was going to tell anyone. I don't care if you're gay or bi but I have a right—"

"You have no rights to my life. None. I don't owe you anything. Say what you want about me but leave him the fuck alone." I held her gaze for a long moment, then turned up the path and started walking.

I passed the econ building, the engineering building, the science building, and kept walking. I couldn't see straight, and my mind had gone from holiday frivolity to a jumbled mess. I didn't know what to do or who to talk to. Not Gabe. Not yet anyway. I had to handle this without freaking him out. I felt so... violated. I couldn't believe Amanda had followed me, and I couldn't believe I hadn't noticed. I'd been looking at Gabe while everyone else had been looking at me. And I'd been perfectly oblivious.

Holy fuck. I may have ruined his life, his career, his—

"Hey, Vaughn. You here to get some extra laps in?" Coach Burton stood at the gate outside the aquatic center.

I looked up in a daze at the familiar signage. I'd walked clear across campus yet somehow, I wasn't surprised. This was my happy place. At least it used to be.

"Um...no. I—"

"Are you okay? You don't look so good."

"Yeah. I—no. No, actually I'm not okay. I'm sick. I'm not gonna make it to practice today."

Coach stepped into my space. He looked more like a worried parent than a badass coach. "Is something bothering you?"

I shook my head emphatically and tried a smile. It wasn't pretty, but I figured I'd get points for effort. "No. Everything's fine," I lied.

"Take care of yourself, Vaughn. We need you."

I inclined my head, then turned to the gate and started moving. And I didn't stop.

BLOCK AFTER BLOCK, through business and residential sections. From good parts to bad parts and back again until I could see the ocean in the distance. It took well over an hour to get home. I didn't mind. I needed the time to think, clear my head, and come up with some sort of plan. By the time I opened my front door, I hoped to have one. I didn't. I was more confused than ever.

No. That was too kind. I was a fucking mess.

I turned off my cell and concentrated on homework and did my best not to stare at my watch, mentally ticking down the minutes until practice began and Gabe realized I hadn't shown up. He'd know something was wrong. *Fuck.* That wasn't cool. I didn't want him to worry. I turned my phone back on and almost dropped it when it lit up like a Christmas tree with texts and voice messages from Chelsea, Troy, Evan...and Amanda. And one from Gabe.

Where r u

I stared at his name on my cell and thought about how to respond. I typed and erased three possible versions of *Everything is cool. Don't worry*, and was putting the finishing touches on a fourth when my doorbell rang. I went perfectly still for a moment and was rewarded with silence, then a nonstop barrage of knocking and ringing.

I jumped off my bed and hurried to answer the door, poised to yell at whoever was standing on the other side. The overzealous junior high schooler selling chocolate bars, the neighbor whose kid threw another ball in my yard, or who wanted to borrow sugar...I was prepared for anything. Except Gabe.

"What are you doing here?"

Gabe set his hands on either side of the doorframe and glowered at me. "I'm looking for you. What the fuck is going on?"

"What do you mean?" I asked, blatantly stalling.

Why was he here? I didn't know what I was doing yet. I didn't have a plan. I only had problems.

Gabe cocked his head. The slight movement was vaguely dangerous. "Coach said you were sick. I guess he saw you and thought you looked pale. Then Troy overheard our conversation and—are you sick?"

"Um...come inside," I said, gesturing for him to enter. I moved into the kitchen and paused in front of the sink. "Do you want some water or something?"

I remembered asking that same question the night he'd brought me home a few months ago. If I hadn't been drunk, I would never have accepted a ride home from him that night. We weren't friends. He was the enemy. My nemesis. He was dangerous. Everyone said so. Yet I'd invited him inside and... everything had changed. I'd changed. Or maybe I'd simply opened my eyes. He'd challenged me and made me aware of a whole new side of myself. One I knew existed but didn't want to face.

And now...I didn't know how to be myself and protect him. I'd been wrong all along. I was the dangerous one.

"No, thanks." Gabe stepped into my space and set his hand on my forehead. "You don't have a fever."

"That's not how you're supposed to read a temperature."

Gabe rolled his eyes. "Fine. Where's your thermometer?

your ass?"

"I'm not sick. I don't need my temperature taken," I said in a low voice.

He crossed his arms and leaned on the counter. His black pullover accentuated his broad shoulders and muscular biceps. I noted the way the late afternoon sun streamed through the window, highlighting his stubbled jaw. Fuck, he was beautiful. I wanted to brush my face against his, pull his arms open and curl against his chest where I belonged. I wanted to block out the excess noise and outside world. They shouldn't have a say here. This was ours. And I wasn't ready for this to end.

"Tell me what's going on, Der."

"Amanda saw us together."

"So...is that a problem? I don't get it."

I huffed incredulously and paced to the refrigerator and back again. "She saw us in your car this morning. She's been following me. She knows about us."

"Oh." He furrowed his brow and then rubbed his chin thoughtfully. "That must be what Troy meant."

I squeezed my eyes shut. "What did he say?"

"Something about seeing you talking with her and...a rumor."

"What kind of rumor?"

"You know...stupid shit people say when two guys spend a lot of time together."

"That we're gay," I supplied, coming to a stop a foot away from him.

I studied his handsome face and saw the fear and longing coalesce. This was new to me, but it wasn't new to Gabe. I felt his pain layered on top of my own. I hated that someone so strong and vibrant had cause to worry about being considered "less than" because of his sexuality. I hated that he'd become accustomed to covering up or downplaying one of the best parts of himself.

"I guess they know about us," he whispered in a faraway tone.

I bit my lip hard enough to taste blood. "This is my fault. I'm so sorry."

Gabe stepped closer and brushed a tear from my cheek. "Hey, don't do that, baby. It's going to be okay."

"How?" I swallowed hard and let out an aggravated sigh.

"Nothing changes. We're just going to do our thing. Go to school, go to practice. We're not gonna worry about it. What we do is no one else's business," he said firmly.

"Yeah, but that's not how it works. And if we weren't at the end of our season and you weren't on the national team, maybe this wouldn't matter." I pushed my hand through my hair in frustration. "She said she wouldn't tell anyone, but I don't trust her. The timing sucks and—"

"The timing is always going to suck." He hollowed out his cheek with his tongue and stared at something beyond my shoulder before refocusing. "But I can't change who I am. I don't know how to do this, though. When you Googled gay sex, did you Google 'how to come out' too?"

I cocked my head curiously. "You want to come out?"

"I don't think I have a choice," he sighed. "Announcing it seems like a lot of work. Maybe I'll just start wearing Pride T-shirts around campus. It'll be a conversation starter. I saw one I kinda liked online that said 'I prefer...' and had a picture of a rooster. I mean, a cock. That oughta—"

"This isn't a joke, Gabe."

"No. But it's also not the end of the world."

"It might be the end of something else."

Gabe narrowed his eyes and gave me a sharp look. "Like what?"

"Everything you've worked for. You can't disrupt your life like that or blow your shot at your dream. It's not right." I took a deep breath before continuing. "Look, I didn't go to practice today because I needed some space to think about what might happen.

My parents will be surprised and confused, but they'll probably be more freaked out about me not working for my dad than being bi. When the season ends, my water polo career is over. If I lose friends, they aren't my real friends anyway. In a few months I'm going to graduate, and everything is going to change again. I have nothing to lose, but you do. I won't stand in your way."

"Are you breaking up with me?" he asked in cocking his head in confusion.

I pursed my lips and swallowed hard. "It's not what I want, but—I can't be with you and act like I don't care. I'm in too deep, Gabe. Sometimes I don't recognize myself. I always thought I was honest to a fault, but I've been living a lie. Maybe I had good reason. It was new and I was scared, and I didn't want to rock the boat. But I can't go on like this, and I can't ask you to give up any portion of your dream for me."

"Hang on." Gabe held his hand up and shook his head. "So... you're coming out, but you don't want me to?"

"Yeah. If Amanda tells anyone she saw us kiss, I'll say it was me coming on to you. Embarrassing for you because we're teammates, blah, blah, blah...but you're a cool guy and you didn't want to hurt my feelings. I'll be last week's news in no time. People will forget me by graduation. And when they talk about you, they'll talk about your killer cross-cage shot and how you're going to kick ass in the next summer Olympics. Not who you sleep with. That's how it should be. And that's what I want for you."

Gabe stared at me for a long moment. "You'd do that for me? Draw attention to yourself and potentially sacrifice your reputation...to save mine?"

"Of course."

"Why?"

"I love you."

We stared at each other in shock for a moment.

Fuck. I hadn't meant to say that out loud. I opened my mouth to downplay the sentiment, but I couldn't do it. I did love him.

Completely and without reservation. And I'd do anything for him.

"Then why do you want me to go?" he asked.

The pain in his voice surprised me. I bit my lip and swiped at a tear in the corner of my eye. "I don't. It's just the way it has to be for now."

"There's got to be another way. I don't want to lose you, Der."

I reached out to tentatively caress his cheek. "You'll never lose me. I'll always be here for you. It'll just be different. For now."

"I don't want different. I want us...the way we are."

"Just for now."

"Der...baby..." He pulled me against his chest and held me tightly.

I clung to his shirt and let out a pained sob. I was afraid to release him, but the weight of our combined pain was almost too much to bear. One of us had to let go.

After a minute or so, I pushed back gently and swiped my hand across my nose when I heard the front door clicked open. Evan's footsteps reverberated on the hardwood flooring. Any second now he'd walk in. Just what I needed.

"You should leave."

Gabe's nostrils flared. He looked angry and upset and on the verge of losing his shit. His eyes were wet with unshed tears. Fuck, he was breaking my heart.

"I'm gonna figure this out. I—I'll find a way. Trust me," he whispered fervently. He held my gaze intently before walking away.

I froze in place. I heard low voices in the next room, but I couldn't make out words above the rush of blood to my head.

What had I done? Was this over? It wasn't right.

I turned abruptly and grunted a greeting when Evan walked into the kitchen. I was aware of him moving behind me. The refrigerator opening, the front door closing. Normal everyday sounds while my world fell to pieces around me. The jarring contrast was so fucking wrong. And why did it suddenly hurt to breathe? I let out a ragged rush of air and tried to pull myself together. Fast. Evan was going to start asking questions any second now and—

"What's not right?" he asked, as if on cue.

I didn't bother turning around. "Huh?"

"You just said, 'It's not right.' Are you okay?"

I shrugged, then headed down the hallway toward my room. Evan moved in front of me and shot his arm out to bar me from entering.

"What are you doing?" I slinked under his arm and pointed my finger, wordlessly asking him to get out.

Because he was Evan, he stepped around me and flopped onto my mattress with an expectant look.

"I'm not leaving until you tell me what's going on," he said matter-of-factly. "What's up with you and Gabe?"

I backed up and leaned against the wall with my arms crossed. "Just water polo stuff. No big deal," I bluffed.

His gaze traveled slowly from my shoes to my face. He made eye contact with me briefly, then looked away. "Will it make it easier if I tell you I already know?"

I opened and closed my mouth twice before moving to my bed. I grabbed my pillow and held it against my chest like a shield, then swallowed hard. *Fuck, could this day possibly get any worse?*

"What do you know?" I croaked, licking my suddenly dry lips.

"You're gay, and he's your boyfriend."

I didn't respond right away. The certainty in his tone made it clear my confirmation was merely a formality. I let out a deep sigh and fell forward, bracing my elbows on my knees.

"Mmm."

"Am I close?"

"Does it matter?" I countered.

"Not to me. It would have been nice to hear it from you instead of—"

"Who told you?"

Evan scrunched his nose and made a funny face. "Nobody told me. I've got ears, dude. I know what sex through the walls sounds like, and I know the only person who comes over regularly is Gabe. It doesn't take a rocket scientist to put the pieces together. So are you...a couple?"

"No."

"Did you just break up?" he asked gently.

"I guess we did." I stared at Evan's scuffed Nikes and willed myself not to break down when tears welled in my eyes.

"Do you want to talk about it?"

"Evan..." I held my breath for a moment, then sighed heavily. "I don't know how to talk to you or anyone about this. Yes, I'm gay or bi or whatever but—"

"That's cool. You know no one really cares anymore, right? I mean, love who you want. Be true to yourself."

"It would be nice if it was that simple," I scoffed.

"Why isn't it? You wouldn't be the first gay or bi athletes to come out. And it might actually help younger people going through the same thing. If you're ready...I guess."

"I don't really have a choice. Amanda cornered me today and I—"

"What'd she say?" Evan's forehead creased indignantly.

I briefly filled Evan in on my confrontation with my ex. "I don't know who she's going to tell or if she'll say anything at all, but I won't let her take my story away from me. It's mine."

"So you're going to come out?"

"Yes."

"And what about Gabe? You aren't doing this alone, are you?" he asked, his forehead creased in confusion.

"Coming out isn't a team sport, Ev. It's personal and it has to feel right and be right and..."

"You're not ready, are you?" Evan whispered.

"No. I'm so fucking scared." I swallowed around the grapefruit in my throat as tears welled in my eyes.

"Hey, it's gonna be okay."

"Maybe....My parents are going to be weird, and my grandmother might not talk to me again. She's super conservative. Then there's my team. Those guys are like brothers to me. Maybe it'll be fine, but you never know. Sometimes people tell you they're cool but they aren't really and"—I paused to suck in a deep breath—"everything's gonna change before I'm ready, and I might lose it all."

"You're not gonna lose me, man. I'm here for you. I always will be." Evan put his arm around me and squeezed my shoulder.

"Thank you."

"I mean it. I'll walk in to that locker room with you and kick ass if I have to. Don't think I won't," he said menacingly.

I chuckled and pushed him away. "I believe you. Thanks, Evan. But I've got this."

WHO WAS I KIDDING? I didn't have shit. I had no idea how to come out. I spent that night Googling coming out stories for ideas. There were so many ways to go about this. I could update my status on social media, post a video on YouTube, write a letter, bake a cake...the options were endless. None of them were for me. I wasn't flashy enough to pull off fabulous. I thought about getting Mitch's number from Chelsea and asking his story, but that would entail so much...talking. If there was a way to do it once and get it over with, I was on board. If not, I had to take one bite at a time. And I might as well start with the hardest piece first.

The following day I put together a short itinerary that went something like this: Skip practice, skip class, eat lunch, make banana bread, skip class and skip practice again. Make a brief appearance at the end of the second practice, come out, field questions. Go to the market, buy chocolate, and eat feelings.

I thought about telling my folks sometime during the day, but it seemed like the kind of message that required a more personal touch. I wasn't sure I could handle an awkward phone conversation in my current headspace anyway. It was better to mentally prepare cutting myself open in front of a fierce group of college-age athletes. My peers, my teammates, my friends. With any luck, I'd still have a few who wouldn't look at me differently when I assured them I was still me. Just a more honest version.

Like it or not, my quest for a new start couldn't begin until I confronted my fear and dishonesty head on. I had so many speeches racing through my head. Hopefully this first one would go well. I sat on a bench under a tree outside the social ecology building and stared at a leaf stuck to the bottom of my shoe. The pointed edges were wilted and torn. I lifted my foot to dislodge it just as a shadow fell over me. I glanced up and nodded a greeting before patting the empty space beside me.

"Hi," I said.

"What do you want, Derek?" Amanda asked in a hollow-sounding tone.

"This is for you." I handed her a loaf of banana bread wrapped in foil.

"You made banana bread." She stared at the seam in the foil for a long moment before looking at me with tears in her eyes.

"I want to apologize. You were right. I owed you the truth. Not yesterday but...in June. I couldn't be honest with you because I wasn't honest with myself. I hurt you and...I'm sorry."

"So you *are* gay."

"I'm bi."

She was quiet for a moment. Then she pushed her long hair over her shoulder and regarded me curiously. "I would have been okay with that. We could have been okay."

"Thanks for saying that, but it's not true."

"It is true. I loved you. And you loved me...at least for a while. If you'd just told me—"

"Mandy, it wasn't that easy. It's taken me a long time to say the word 'bi' out loud. I wasn't ready then, and I couldn't have been the real me with you until I was out. I guess our timing was off. That's my fault. You said you agreed we were over, but I should have noticed that you weren't. I should have been more sensitive. I fucked up. I'm sorry. I was too self-absorbed. I didn't mean to be callous or cruel. And I never meant to hurt you. I swear. I want you to be happy. You'll find the right guy. I'm sorry it's not me."

"Oh, Derek." Amanda threw herself into my arms and sniffed. I closed my eyes and held her close while she cried.

I felt bad I'd caused her sorrow, but I didn't love her in the same way, at the same time, or to the same degree. Perhaps our story would have been different if I'd been braver. But then I wouldn't have known Gabe the way I did now. And I wouldn't have acknowledged the other part of me. I'd still be in the dark.

Now I was something closer to free.

At four fifteen I strode purposefully into the empty locker room. I didn't have a workout bag with me today. No towel, no Speedo...nothing that marked me as "one of the guys." I wasn't part of a team at the moment. I was alone in the deep end, hoping I remembered how to swim when this was over.

I headed for my locker out of habit as Eminem pumped me up and encouraged me to lose myself and seize my moment. I bopped my head to the beat and let the cadence build as I paced around the row of benches. Up one side, down the next. *You got this. You can do this.* I raised my fist in the air as I rounded a metal bench for another lap and ran into a brick wall or a—

"What are you doing here?" I asked. "You should be in the pool."

Gabe fastened his towel around his waist and shook the

excess water from his hair, then locked his gaze on me. The intensity in his stare overwhelmed me. It was like he was speaking without words, but I couldn't understand him with my head whirling in twenty directions at once. I ripped my earbuds out and stuffed them into my sweatshirt pocket and motioned for him to answer.

"I *was* in the pool. I saw you walk in." He paused as he stepped closer to me. "And I wanted to talk you. Alone."

"Oookay."

"Der, I know what you're going to do and—"

"Don't try to stop me," I warned, narrowing my gaze. "I won't mention your name at all. I promise. But this is important to me. It's something I need to do. I've been up all night asking myself if this mattered. I could blow off any rumor Amanda started and pretend to be insulted anyone would suggest I'm gay. But I don't want to live like that. I'm not giving her or anyone else the upper hand. I won't let them say I'm less than or unworthy. I'm not," I hissed.

Gabe raised his hands in surrender and gave a lopsided grin. "I know who you are. And I won't try to stop you. I love you, Der."

I cocked my head. "Love?"

He closed the distance between us until he stood directly in front of me. Bare feet next to a pair of black and white Vans. My fully clothed state should have given me some sort of advantage, but I'd never felt more vulnerable in my life.

"Yes. I love you. And I did some thinking too. I—" He glanced toward the door and then back at me. "Shoot. They're coming. We can talk after. Just know that whatever you say, I'm on your side, baby."

I furrowed my brow in confusion when he stepped away just as the rest of our team filed into the locker room.

"Hey, Vaughn. What's your deal? If you're sick, stay the fuck away from me, man," Troy said, offering me a fist bump anyway.

"I'm fine," I assured him.

I greeted a few more of the guys and then jumped on a bench and whistled loudly to get everyone's attention. No one looked alarmed or even curious. After practice powwows were a norm. They probably thought I'd popped in to give a team pep talk and remind everyone to keep playing hard even though I'd basically taken two days off. I had maybe three minutes before they were itching to head to the showers and get the fuck out of here.

I cast my gaze over the dozen or so guys looking my way. "Um...I have something to tell you. I had a speech but honestly, I forgot half of it. I've known most of you for years. You guys are my brothers. I care about you and I hope we stay in touch after graduation and—"

"What the fuck? Are you quitting?" Jason asked.

I shook my head in response. "No, I'm not quitting. I'm not sick. I'm not going anywhere and there's nothing wrong. I'm..." I swallowed hard around the instant wave of nausea before blurting, "I'm gay. Actually, I'm bi. And I just...I wanted you to hear it from me. Any questions?"

Silence. I wasn't sure if that was a relief or cause for concern. Then someone cleared his throat behind me.

"Yeah. Will you go out with me?"

I jumped from the bench and turned to face Gabe. What the hell was he doing? "Why would I go out with you?"

" 'Cause I have a crush on you and I happen to be bi too," Gabe replied matter-of-factly.

"He's being an asshole." Troy stepped between us and shot a warning look at Gabe before turning to me. "Don't listen to him. Hey, gay, straight, white, black, any color in between, including polka dot...you're one of us. We got your back, man."

"I do too." Gabe pushed Troy aside and moved in front of me. He'd changed into a pair of sweats that hung low on his hips. His abs were a thing of beauty. Fuck...he was gorgeous. He gave me a wicked nervous smile, then pulled a white T-shirt over his head and smoothed it over his chest so I could clearly see "Out and

Proud" emblazoned in rainbow lettering on the front. "I couldn't find the cock shirt but I figured this'll do. Hey, I may be an asshole sometimes, but I'm one hundred percent serious. I'm with you, Der. We're not waiting for the right time. We're going to *make it* right. And if you're diving into the deep end, I'm coming with you."

I grinned and pulled him into a hug. I kept it brief. I'd said what I'd needed to say. It was time to go. The room broke into a flurry of gasps and hoots followed by a round of raucous cheering when Gabe followed me out of the locker room.

We walked side by side onto the pool deck and out the gate. Gabe grabbed my wrist when we reached a tall hedge. It wasn't much but it provided a modicum of privacy between the parking lot and the aquatics center.

"Did we just come out?" he asked in an awed tone.

I nodded, smiling at the wonderment in his voice before pulling him against me and crashing my mouth over his. I held him close, reveling in his nearness. When we broke for air, I rested my forehead against his for a moment.

"You weren't supposed to do that, Gabe."

"But it felt right. I was thinking about it last night and...being out scares the shit out of me, but being without you...that sounds like hell. I can't do that."

"What about the national team and going to the Olympics and your family?"

"My mom will be fine. My dad won't be, but that's his problem. I seriously doubt I'll lose my place on the team. They need me. But I'm willing to work harder than ever to prove myself. Because truth matters. We matter. But if I never get a shot at gold, I'd still be a winner. Nothing else matters if I can't have you, Der."

"That's so...goofy," I said, unable to keep the emotion from my voice.

Gabe laughed and brushed a tear from the corner of my eye. "It's true, though. In a way, I've been thinking about it my whole life, plotting and planning the right time and the right way to deliver my message. It's no one's business, and it pisses me off that we're put in a position of having to explain ourselves. But you...you didn't hesitate. That's so fucking brave. I don't know anyone else like you. You're a quiet, courageous leader with a big heart, and I'm loud and cocky and I like things done my way. But somehow we fit. And I knew from the moment we met, you were special. I didn't know you'd be mine but you are. I can't let you go now."

"I love you," I whispered as I tilted my head and fused my lips against his.

We clung to each other in the shadows for a long moment. Then he slipped his hand into mine, and we headed for the parking lot. No one looked our way. No one seemed to care about the two guys holding hands. For most people, this was an average Wednesday. For me, it was the biggest day of my life. Sure, I was nervous as hell. Neither of us knew what the future held. We hadn't solved any major problems or conquered the world...yet. But we were in this together. And this felt like a promising place to begin.

EPILOGUE

"There is no greatness where simplicity, goodness, and truth are absent."—Leo Tolstoy, *War and Peace*

THE GREAT LAWN outside the aquatics center was a beautiful venue for graduation. The weather forecast called for warmer than average spring temperatures and clear skies. But sitting outside on an eighty-degree day for a two-plus hour ceremony was brutal. Thankfully, I'd lucked out. The university divided matriculation by majors, and my class scored a nine a.m. start time. If all went according to plan, Gabe and I would have a couple of hours alone after brunch with my parents and before the real parties began tonight.

I glanced out at the sea of black gowns and graduation caps to the general seating for family and friends behind us. They'd just ushered the row in front of me toward the makeshift stage. I was next. I was about to become a college graduate. I'd fulfilled the requirements for my major with top honors. Not an easy feat while playing a competitive sport but I'd done it. It was a great achievement but quite honestly, I was far more excited about some of the other things I'd accomplished in the past few months. I was an out-and-proud athlete with an amazing boyfriend, a supportive group of friends, and exciting plans for the future.

I'd enrolled in a culinary school in LA that was set to begin in the fall. The commute from Long Beach would suck, but it was only twice a week. I also had a part-time job lined up at an exclusive oceanfront restaurant I hoped would give me some real-life kitchen and business experience before I attempted to open my own bistro. The next stage would require as much hard work and dedication as the past five years, but I was ready for it.

And so was Gabe. He'd moved into my place last weekend. His lease was up at his apartment at the end of the month but he had a big tournament to prepare for, so we'd decided it was better to get it over with. My parents were charging a nominal fee for rent in deference to my newly graduated status. It wasn't free but was still a hell of a lot cheaper than anything we could afford in the area. In a way, I think the gesture was an olive branch of sorts.

I came out to my folks during the holidays. They weren't thrilled with what they referred to as my "life choices." But as I'd suspected, they were more freaked out about me attending culinary school than having a boyfriend. They thought I was nuts. Maybe I was but damn, it felt good. At some point they must have noticed I was happier than ever, because they slowly thawed and began to try to understand me on my terms. They'd started showing up to Gabe's games, and they'd even invited his mom and him to brunch today.

The family drama hadn't been as intense as either of us feared. Gabe's mom welcomed me warmly when he introduced me as his boyfriend and his dad...well, he was kind of a jerk. He shook my hand but then proceeded to ignore me. I didn't think he had a problem with our relationship, though. I just wasn't interesting to him once I hung up my water polo cap. The game was more important.

Thankfully, Gabe didn't feel the same way. He worked hard, but he kept perspective. He wanted to ride out his success in the pool and go as far as it would take him. However, he was committed to finishing his degree too. Maybe he'd help run my bistro or maybe he'd start a swim program for underprivileged kids. The sky was the limit, I mused as I made my way along the grassy path.

I counted the graduates in front of me, patiently waiting for my name to be called. Three, two, one...

"...Derek Jackson Vaughn..."

I shook hands with the proctor and accepted the certificate he handed over before heading back down the path. I waved toward my friends hollering my name a few yards away, then stopped in my tracks and flashed a huge smile at the gorgeous man standing at the end of the row.

"Congratulations."

Gabe pulled me into his arms for a hearty embrace and then released me. It was a safe hug. Anyone around us would have assumed we were just friends, especially on a day like today when hugs were a dime a dozen. But why settle for ordinary when you could have something memorable? I cupped the back of his neck and sealed my mouth over his in a kiss no one would mistake as "friendly."

I chuckled when Gabe pushed his sunglasses up on his head and blinked theatrically when we broke for air.

"Thank you," I said with a laugh.

"Did I tell you I'm proud of you?"

"I think so, but feel free to say it again," I teased.

Gabe gave me a lopsided grin and nodded. "I'm proud of you, Der. And I can't wait to see what kind of bread and spaghetti and —what else are you putting on your menu?"

"That's it. Just bread and spaghetti. Everything else is overkill."

"So true. I love you, baby."

"I love you too."

Gabe threw his arm over my shoulder and gathered me to his side. He kissed my temple sweetly and gave me a side-eyed look filled with humor and love and hope. It was moments like that I knew without a doubt I was where I was supposed to be. I wasn't afraid anymore. I was free. There was a sense of personal contentment in truth. Somehow, I knew Gabe and I were out of the deep and on the right path...in love.

OUT IN THE END ZONE - COMING OCTOBER 2018

EXCERPT FROM OUT IN THE END ZONE BY LANE HAYES (OCTOBER 2018)

The challenge in Mitch's gaze was filled with humor. I had a feeling he didn't expect much from me on this project. He'd probably script easygoing dialogue and throw in a random kiss to throw people off. No doubt I was his third or fourth choice, filling in for someone else...like Rory. In fact, I was suddenly sure of it and the idea pissed me off for no good reason at all. His lack of confidence and my niggling sense of misplaced jealousy made me want to surprise the hell out him.

"Okay, fine." I wiped my mouth then stood abruptly and moved to his side.

Mitch looked up at me and frowned. "Are you leaving?"

"No."

"Then wha—"

I cupped his face in my hands and pressed my lips against his.

The kiss was meant to shut him up and throw him off stride. And okay, maybe I hoped he'd forget his name for half a second and realize I should have always been his first choice. A harmless kiss to seal the deal seemed like a good way to counteract negativity and prove I was fully onboard.

But I hadn't counted on his lips being so damn soft. I sank

into the connection and lost myself for a moment. He was sweet and seductive and fuck, he felt amazing. I wanted to taste him and smell him. I rubbed my thumbs over his jaw and sucked on his lower lip to keep myself from pushing my tongue inside his mouth. The desire was real but my timing was off.

I backed up slowly and moved to my chair with a lopsided smile I hoped exuded confidence I didn't feel. It could have been a total fail. Mitch's shocked expression didn't bode well. I had to say something. Anything.

"How was that?" I winced. Fuck, that was lame.

"*What* was that?" he asked, touching two fingers to his bottom lip.

"A boyfriend kiss. The spontaneous in public kind that should convince the average passerby that I'm into you. How'd I do?"

Mitch nodded slowly and absently reached for his water. "Very very well. You're hired," he deadpanned.

I busted up laughing and held my hand out for a high five. "Gee thanks."

"I appreciate this, Evan. I know I'm asking a lot. More than the average friend of a friend should. If you want to think about it and get back to me tomorrow or—"

"Let's not overthink this. It's an assignment or a friend helping a friend." I pulled my wallet out of my pocket and set my credit card over the leather folder the waiter left between us. "The way I see it, life is short. I don't want to be cautious or careful and I don't want to say no to any challenge that comes along. When I die, I want to know I lived. That's all."

Mitch nodded slowly. "Okay. Well, next step... we need to go over a schedule. We'll have to rehearse before we film for the first time. We need to check lighting, angles and go over material. And we'll have to plan a few appearances. Nothing major. A trip to a coffee shop will work. Be prepared for selfie central. If your selfie game is weak, I can give you pointers. I'll create a joint account for us on other platforms, like Instagram. Do you have Instagram?"

I shook my head and chuckled at his flabbergasted expression. "I don't have time. I barely check Facebook."

"Oh boy. I'll handle it. And not to worry, I won't post anything without your approval."

"I trust you, Mitch."

"Thanks. For everything. I think we're about to do something amazing. I can't wait," he gushed.

We shared a smile that felt like a handshake or signing our names on a dotted line side by side. Or some version of a commitment that came with a virtual eraser. This wasn't binding. It was just for fun. A new way to push old boundaries and to remind myself that complacency was a form of death. And I wasn't giving in or giving up until I'd done it all.

ABOUT THE AUTHOR

Lane Hayes is grateful to finally be doing what she loves best. Writing full-time! It's no secret Lane loves a good romance novel. An avid reader from an early age, she has always been drawn to well-told love story with beautifully written characters. These days she prefers the leading roles to both be men. Lane discovered the M/M genre a few years ago and was instantly hooked. Her debut novel was a 2013 Rainbow Award finalist and subsequent books have received Honorable Mentions, and were First Place winners in the 2016 and 2017 Rainbow Awards. She loves red wine, chocolate and travel (in no particular order). Lane lives in Southern California with her amazing husband in a newly empty nest.

*Be sure to join Lane's reading group, Lane's Lovers, on Facebook for immediate updates!

www.lanehayes.wordpress.com

ALSO BY LANE HAYES

Made in the USA
Columbia, SC
07 September 2018